Sumr
Sewing Bee

De-ann Black

Published 2017

Summer Sewing Bee

ISBN: 9781521743379

Also by De-ann Black (Romance, Crime/Thrillers & Children's books). See her Amazon Author page or website for further details about her books, illustrations, art and fabric designs. www.De-annBlack.com

Romance:
The Chocolatier's Cottage
Christmas Cake Chateau
The Beemaster's Cottage
The Sewing Bee By The Sea
The Flower Hunter's Cottage
The Christmas Knitting Bee
The Sewing Bee & Afternoon Tea
The Tea Shop
The Vintage Sewing & Knitting Bee
Shed In The City
The Bakery By The Seaside
Champagne Chic Lemonade Money
The Christmas Chocolatier
The Christmas Tea Shop & Bakery
The Vintage Tea Dress Shop In Summer
The Fairytale Tea Dress Shop In Edinburgh
Oops! I'm The Paparazzi
The Bitch-Proof Suit
The Cure For Love
The Tea Dress Shop At Christmas

Crime/Thrillers:
Electric Shadows. The Strife Of Riley. Shadows Of Murder.

Children's books:
Faeriefied. Secondhand Spooks. Poison-Wynd. Wormhole Wynd. Science Fashion. School For Aliens.

Colouring books:
Summer Garden. Spring Garden. Autumn Garden. Sea Dream. Festive Christmas. Christmas Garden. Flower Bee. Wild Garden. Faerie Garden Spring. Flower Hunter. Stargazer Space. Bee Garden. Festive Christmas Colouring Book Journal.

Contents

CHAPTER ONE

Sewing in Scotland

'Do you think it would be feasible to make our wee main street look like Los Angeles?'

Ibbie's face was a picture of hope mixed with mischief. She was up to something. She was often up to something. Daphne had barely stepped inside the little knitting shop when she hit her with the question. Ibbie's laptop was open on the shop counter and whatever was on the screen looked very razzle–dazzle. Yes, she was definitely up to something.

'No,' said Daphne.

Daphne went over to the counter, a rose stencilled, pale blue dresser with drawers stocked with yarn. Daphne's dressmaking shop had a similar counter only hers was painted cream and filled with sewing trims. She enjoyed their end of the week chit–chats when both their shops were closed on a Saturday evening and they could indulge in a glass or two of wine or a cup of tea. Tonight, Daphne had brought a bramble and buttercream cake with her to share.

Their shops were situated next door to each other in the little Scottish coastal town's main street. Ibbie's knitting shop window displayed a fantastic selection of yarn and was draped with summer bunting. Daphne's beautiful dress and fabric shop was where the local sewing bee was abuzz on Wednesday evenings and Sunday afternoons.

Both shop fronts were painted cream and had a modern vintage look, sandwiched between a bakery and a bookshop. Nearby was a quilt shop, cafe, tea shop, hairdressing salon, bar restaurant, traditional pubs and all sorts of quaint shops dotted along the town's main thoroughfare.

'Yes, but—'

'No, Ibbie. There's no way to make our main street look anything remotely like Los Angeles. For a start, our main street is. . . and I don't want to diss where we live because I love it here, but it's what some people refer to as blink and you'll miss it. Los Angeles is

1

a metropolis of glamour — a sprawling city of glistening lights. See the difference? Huge city versus wee town. No comparison.'

Ibbie sighed and poured a glass of wine. The disappointment showed on her pretty features. The petulant lip. The slump of her shoulders. As if it was Daphne's fault for dashing her hopes of whatever she'd wanted to meddle in.

They'd been friends since school. Now in their early thirties, Ibbie was still roping Daphne into her madcap schemes.

Daphne was determined not to get involved or encourage her. It had been a hectic day, a busy first week in June. With their shops closed for the night, all Daphne wanted to do was drop in for their usual glass of wine or cuppa and a natter. They were both so occupied with their shops that these precious evenings were the only chance they got to relax and exchange local gossip. Despite living in a small town on the West Coast of Scotland that barely made its way on to any map, there was never a shortage of gossip and scandal. Not in this town.

Daphne headed through to the back of the shop to make the tea. 'I brought a cake from Nairna's bakery. She says it's got extra brambles and buttercream. Want a slice with a cup of tea?'

'Yes, this wine is rotten.'

The kettle boiled and Daphne set the cups up with milk. She gazed out the window at the back garden. Ibbie had pinned solar fairy lights across the lawn and they flickered in the twilight.

The two–storey buildings were houses converted decades ago into shop premises. They both lived above their respective shops. Sometimes Daphne felt as if she never stopped working. Evenings were spent catching up on sewing and dealing with online orders for the fabric and dresses she sold. Some of the dresses were vintage and others were new, sewn by Daphne. She loved making the dresses more than anything.

They both earned money from their online sales and from local trade.

Daphne had a knack for sourcing beautiful fabrics, from pretty cotton prints to silks and chiffon. She had a great range of threads and sewing accessories, and part of her shop was like a haberdashery. She held a sewing bee in the shop which was popular with those who enjoyed everything from dressmaking to quilting.

2

They shared patterns, sewing techniques and gossip while indulging in tea and cakes.

Ibbie's selection of yarns attracted knitters from the local area and her online sales were excellent. She sold knitting supplies and patterns as well as lovely yarn.

Each shop had a front window looking on to the street, and their window displays often complemented each other. Ibbie would borrow one of Daphne's dresses and put it on her mannequin along with a knitted cardigan to advertise her yarn. Likewise, Daphne would drape a hand–knitted shawl around one of her dresses, promoting that the shawl was made from Ibbie's yarn and could be purchased next door.

Daphne had two mannequins in her window and although both their shops were small, they'd made the most of the space available and frequently changed their displays to entice further trade. When Daphne purchased her mannequins second–hand from a wholesaler who dealt in classic shop fittings, it was a coincidence that one was a glamorous blonde and the other one titian. People often did a double–take thinking it was Daphne and Ibbie in the windows, especially as the redhead had a mischievous expression and the blonde's blue eyes and attractive features resembled their owner.

'A big slice of cake?' Daphne called through to her.

'Yes, I'm starving. I couldn't be fused making a dinner, and there was a queue at the chip shop. Duncan was there with his new girlfriend so I didn't bother waiting. She had a ring on her engagement finger. Bastard.'

Daphne brought the tea and cake through on a tray. She set it down on the counter. Two large cups brim full and slices of cake.

'You're well rid of him.'

Ibbie nodded reluctantly. 'She's got a rotten attitude.'

'They're a well–matched couple.'

Ibbie's sad expression broke into a grin. 'They are, aren't they?' She took a gulp of her tea. 'You're right. I'm well rid of him.'

Daphne sat down and bit into her cake, enjoying the delicious buttercream and brambles.

Ibbie glanced at the laptop screen and then at Daphne.

Daphne pretended not to notice.

'You want to know why I asked about Los Angeles, don't you?'

Daphne shook her head.

'Yes you do.'

'I really don't.'

'Awe come on, Daphne. At least let me tell you about it.'

'Give me the short course.'

'Okay. . .what happened was, I was looking at the Hollywood website that I read every week. The one with the glamorous gossip and stuff.'

Ibbie loved films and all the celebrity news and gossip. Sometimes she'd tell Daphne snippets from the website.

'Well. . .' Ibbie continued, 'I was reading the latest news and that's when I saw this.' She pointed to the screen. 'It was listed with the advertisements and marked URGENT. I couldn't resist, so I clicked on the link and here's the gist of what it said — one of the top directors in Hollywood got stuffed for a prime location for the film he's making and put out an urgent call for an alternative location. The film is set in Los Angeles. It's a romantic thriller starring one of my heartthrobs — Shaw Starlight. So I thought—'

'Nope.'

'It's mainly night shoots. It says so. Anywhere can look like anywhere at night when it's dark.'

'The lights in Los Angeles are spectacular in comparison to what we've got in our street. And this is Scotland. It looks nothing like L.A.'

'You've never been there.'

'Neither have you.'

'No, but I've studied it. I've read about it. And it's mainly shots of the street at night with people faffing about. We've got plenty of lights from the pubs, and I know the woman at the tea shop would be happy to put twinkle lights in her window to add some pizzazz to the street. Lots of other shops and businesses would get involved if they knew that a Hollywood film was going to be made here. The cafe has lights. And your ex–boyfriend has those cathodes for his computers. He could put them in the windows. It's feasible.'

'It's not.'

'This is the email I was thinking about sending to the director's assistant.'

'Email? You've written an email?'

'I haven't sent it. I was just. . .awe come on, Daphne. I sometimes like to think what life would be like if we lived over there with all the stars. I know it's pie in the sky. I know that, but sometimes it's nice to dream, especially when we get dumped by men with shitty attitudes. Duncan was a prat and so was your ex–boyfriend.'

There was no arguing with that.

Daphne leaned over and read the email. Ibbie had pitched it well.

'The requirements are that they need a street with lights, and people walking up and down to film some end scenes. They also need a lovely beach, preferably a sandy bay with a clear view out to the sea. Oh and an airport. I've attached photos of the shore from a sunny day last year, pictures of the airport, and the main street when it was all lit up with fairy lights last Christmas. Our two shops looked great. That Christmas tree you had in your front window glowed like a beacon. Three sets of fairy lights seemed excessive but it worked. The party dresses were all lit up, especially the cocktail dresses with hundreds of sequins. Very glamorous. Your dresses could give L.A. some competition.'

Daphne smiled as she gazed at the pictures. 'I'd forgotten about those photos we took down the shore. It was a scorcher of a day. We did the right thing locking the shops up at lunchtime and sticking up notices saying we're away down the shore to enjoy ourselves. Two bottles of lemonade, grab a couple of swimsuits from the stock and off we went.'

She'd given Ibbie the red and white polka dot swimsuit that added curves to her friend's slight frame. The red should've clashed with her titian hair, but Ibbie wore colours that emphasised her colouring rather than played it down. Daphne wore the blue halter neck. Height–wise, Daphne was marginally taller at five–five but both of them were on the slender side.

Ibbie pointed to one of the swimsuit pictures. 'Your hair looked great, Daphne. Your natural blonde always lightens in the summer. You could give those Beverly Hills blondes a run for their money.'

Daphne looked at her, starting to reconsider things.

Ibbie continued her spiel. 'The town's a postage stamp. No one ever knows it exists, but here we are with a street full of wee shops, a beautiful bay with miles of sea out to the islands, and the airport further along the coast. Let's send the email. What harm would it do?'

'Plenty if things go wrong.'

Ibbie looked almost teary as she said, 'I'd just like to get a reply from them. They're going to tell me to get stuffed, but it would be a reply all the way from Hollywood. To know that someone in a film studio read my message and replied would mean a lot to me. I could print it out and stick it on the shop wall. Customers would come in just to see it.'

A man opened the shop door, popped his head in and called over to them. 'I saw you were in and thought I'd ask, have you got a bicycle pump handy?'

Daphne dealt with him.

'Wait a minute and I'll have a look through the yarn and knitting patterns. Nope no bicycle pump. Maybe it's on the shelf with the crochet accessories? No. Out of luck.'

'Oh very funny,' he muttered and scurried off.

Daphne locked the door behind him.

Ibbie got up and went through to the back of the shop. 'I've got a couple of cans of beer in the fridge and a bottle of cider. We can make cocktails.'

After the potent mix, Daphne was more amenable to the idea. 'What else does it say in the advert?'

'They want to bring a film crew to shoot several night scenes. The street needs to look vibrant but moody. I'm guessing they're doing some of the romance scenes or the leading lady in jeopardy stuff at night.'

'The local authorities would have to give their permission,' said Daphne.

John came padding through from his cat basket. Ibbie had knitted him a new blanket and he'd been sleeping for most of the day. He was a scrapper and his fur was uneven where bits had been torn out in fights with other cats and dogs. There was nothing cute about John except his love of snuggling up close to those he adored unaware how ragged he was.

John strutted in as if his fur was silky smooth instead of mangy and patchwork. His tail was particularly uneven. They weren't sure, as they'd never measured his tail, but Ibbie thought he had a bit missing from the tip and that it was shorter than when he'd first invited himself to stay in her shop when she'd opened it three years ago.

Ibbie lifted John up and he snuggled into her. 'I gave my auntie at the council offices a tinkle, just in case I went ahead with this, and she said that the council would jump at the chance to have a Hollywood film made here. It would finally put us on the map. The film company would probably pay us for the use of the street. And it would boost tourism. My auntie mentioned it to her boss and he was over the moon about the opportunity.'

Daphne sighed. 'Okay, let's say for the sake of argument that everyone here is hunky–dory about the film crew coming over to our town. But it's still a million to one shot that they'd want to film here. It's nothing like Los Angeles, Ibbie. Nothing like it at all.'

Ibbie's elfin features showed her disappointment. 'You're right, Daphne. I was an eejit for even thinking it.'

They downed the dregs of their beer can cocktails and Daphne helped Ibbie stock the shelves with the delivery of yarn that had arrived earlier and hadn't been unpacked.

Ibbie arranged the new summery yarns according to colour, tidied the shop and tried to think happy thoughts.

As she draped a sample of the latest turquoise blue yarn in the window display, Duncan and his new fiancée walked past the shop on their way to one of the pubs.

'Pretend you don't notice him,' Daphne whispered to Ibbie.

'He never looks in these days anyway.'

Daphne and Ibbie feigned being busy while having a sly look at Duncan going by. His fiancée linked her arm through his and behind his back she stuck a finger up at Ibbie.

'Why that wee shi—'

Daphne strong–armed Ibbie behind the knitting display. 'Don't react. That's what she wants.'

Ibbie's cheeks burned fiery pink. 'I'm not letting her away with that. I'm going to kick her arse.' John was at her heels as back–up.

Daphne barred Ibbie from running out the shop to confront her rival. 'She's engaged to Duncan. That's punishment enough for any woman.'

Ibbie peered at them walking away along the street and laughed. 'Aye, you're right, Daph.'

John wound himself around Ibbie's ankles and purred loudly.

Ibbie gave him a ball of wool to play with while Daphne put the kettle on for another cup of tea.

7

John pounced on the wool, grabbed it in his front paws and scarted hell out of it with his claws.

Ibbie gazed at him. 'I know how you feel, John. I know exactly how you feel.'

They chatted for a couple of hours and then Daphne washed the cups, put her cardigan on and got ready to leave.

'Are you coming to the sewing bee tomorrow afternoon?' said Daphne.

'Yes, I'll bring my knitting.'

Ibbie wasn't into sewing, but she liked to join in with the bee. It was always a cheery afternoon of tea and chit–chat.

'Great, see you tomorrow.'

Daphne headed next door into her own shop. The night was warm and lots of sunny days were forecast for June and July.

She went upstairs and gazed out her bedroom window overlooking the main street. A few stragglers were heading home from the pubs. Even with the lights shining on the pavements, it looked nothing like Los Angeles. She closed the curtains and felt glad that Ibbie had abandoned her wild notion of contacting Hollywood.

Next morning, Daphne was up early and made breakfast in the kitchen that felt cosy no matter what time of year it was. Sunlight shone through the yellow flower print curtains she'd made that always gave a glow to the kitchen. She'd painted the cupboards vanilla cream. Other items such as the bread bin and cushion covers for the two wooden chairs and tablecloth were a mix of floral and cream tones. The decor of the living room and bedroom had a similar theme, with chintz curtains, quilted throws on the bed and sofa, and colours ranging from pale blues to soft pinks. She'd sewn most of the accessories herself. The living room and bathroom were at the rear of the house and had a view of the garden's small lawn surrounded with flowers, and a shed.

The sewing bee was held downstairs in the room at the back of the shop. It was kitted out with tables, chairs, sewing machines and shelves stacked with fabric. The shop's decor was similar to her house upstairs with light and airy cream hues blended with florals. Patio doors led out to the garden. On sunny days the sewing bee ladies often sat outside.

It started at 2:30 p.m. on the Sunday afternoon. Daphne had everything ready including a pile of fabric scraps for the quilters. She kept her off–cuts of material for the bee members who stitched them into quilts or other craft projects.

Butterfly cakes and cupcakes topped with buttercream frosting were arranged on cake stands along with shortbread.

The ladies started to arrive on time as the kettle boiled, most bringing cakes and scones with them. Daphne supplied tea and cake, but contributing to the baking was part of the enjoyment.

'I brought chocolate éclairs and cream meringues.' Effie set them on one of the cake stands while other ladies organised the tables and chairs. Effie, a fresh–faced woman in her mid–fifties, had worked as a seamstress before setting up a sewing and craft business in her cottage, and was known for her delicious home baking. Several members added scones, cakes and dainty sandwiches to the buffet. Cups and saucers rattled as the tea was ready to pour. Everyone helped and there was a happy atmosphere to the bee.

Daphne opened the patio doors and the warm afternoon breeze wafted in along with the scent of the garden flowers, especially the sweet peas, lily of the valley, lavender and heliotrope, and mixed with a hint of sea air.

A sewing machine whirred into action along the seams of a floral skirt made from a cotton fabric printed with a flower design in soft blues, pinks and lilacs that was a fair match for the sweet peas. It was one of Daphne's new fabrics.

Florie, owner of the quilt shop nearby, helped two members piece together a quilt using scraps of Daphne's pink bunting print fabric. Florie was thirty, attractive and loved passing on her quilting skills to others. Her grandmother, Ivy, taught her to sew from an early age, and she'd recently fulfilled her dream of owning her own quilt shop. Florie had inherited Ivy's blue eyes and summer blonde hair along with a love of sewing.

'I brought the cocktail dress I'm making,' said June, a brunette in her early thirties who worked at a local bakery. 'I thought I could sew the sequins and beads on. Have you any more of these sequins?'

'Yes, I've plenty in the shop.' Daphne helped June choose the sequins and thread. June joined the bee the previous year as a complete beginner and was now making her own dresses.

'I love the cocktail dresses you sew,' June told Daphne. 'Seeing that sparkly gold dress you had in the window put me in the notion to make one. Goodness knows when I'll ever wear it.'

'You could wear it to the summer ball,' Daphne suggested, 'or put it away until Christmas and the party season.'

June nodded. 'It would be handy for Christmas. I've always wanted something glamorous like this hanging in my wardrobe. Everything I have is so practical.'

'What we need is a girls night out, go dancing and put our glad rags on,' said Effie. 'There are party nights at the hotel. We could go to one of those.'

'And maybe meet some hunky men,' one of the women chipped–in.

June scoffed. 'Chance would be a fine thing. I'm not saying the men around here aren't hunky, but most of them are taken.'

'Hew is single,' said Effie. 'He's in his mid–thirties, ideal for you. You could do worse than get involved with a hotel owner.'

'I admit he's nice, but he's only interested in one woman in this town.' June motioned to Daphne.

Daphne continued sorting the sequins.

'Don't you fancy him?' Effie asked her.

'No, I never have,' Daphne admitted.

'He's a fine, handsome man,' said Effie. 'And he's taken over his father's hotel and done wonders with it. Someone will snap him up.'

'Won't be me,' said Daphne.

Effie shook her head in dismay. 'I never understood what you saw in that ex–boyfriend of yours, the computer technician or whatever it was he did.'

'I thought he was intelligent and we could have interesting conversations,' Daphne explained. 'Unfortunately all he wanted to talk about was computers.'

Effie grinned. 'But he'd nae muscles.'

This was true.

'Do you think Hew has muscles?' Florie tried to sound nonchalant.

'Ooooh!' June pointed at Florie. 'Have you got a fancy for him?'

Florie blushed. 'No, I was just wondering. He's always wearing a suit. Very smart looking, but it's hard to tell if he's. . . fit.'

Daphne shrugged. 'He's tall and rangy, and he looks okay in a suit.'

'More than okay,' said Effie. 'I think he's unfairly overlooked by the local ladies.'

The ladies nodded in agreement.

'I see Duncan has put a ring on his new girlfriend's finger,' said June.

'He didn't waste any time,' said Florie. 'Ibbie is better off without him.'

'How is she taking the engagement news?' Effie asked Daphne.

'Not bad.' Daphne told them what happened the previous night.

'You should've let her kick her arse,' said Effie.

Daphne disagreed. 'Duncan's not worth fighting over.'

'Here's Ibbie now,' Florie whispered, seeing her run past the shop window.

Ibbie came hurrying in carrying her knitting bag. A tangle of yarn spilled out the top like spaghetti. Her ponytail was squiffy, and she looked like she'd thrown on anything she'd grabbed from her wardrobe. Ibbie had the personality and elfin features to suit an eclectic mix of colours and fashion styles, but her clothes were outlandish even by her standards.

'Sorry, I'm running a bit late.' She smiled at Daphne, and then a guilty expression crossed her face.

Daphne pulled her aside. 'Are you okay, Ibbie?'

'Yes, yes, fine,' she said breathlessly. 'I just need a cup of tea.' Then she became silent.

'Are you worried about your knitting?' Daphne eyed the mess of yarn.

'Och, I was trying to knit earlier, but I got my needles in a fankle and the pattern went all to hell.'

Daphne knew something was wrong. Ibbie could knit while watching an entire film on the telly and not drop a stitch.

'Is there something you're not telling me?'

'No, I want to have a lovely time at the bee. It's always a good laugh.'

Silence again.

'Right, what is it?' Daphne demanded.

Wide green eyes stared at her innocently. 'What's what?'

'This is me you're talking to. You're up to something. Or there's something you're not telling me.'

'There's nothing—'

'Spit it out!'

'Okay, so there might be something. When I tell you, promise you won't hit the roof. It wasn't my fault. Really, it wasn't.'

CHAPTER TWO

Dressmaking and Cupcakes

'John sent the email to Hollywood?' Daphne shrieked. 'The cat?'

'It was an accident. He likes to snooze on the laptop and he must've pressed the send button with his paws.'

Some of the women stared, wondering what was happening.

Ibbie waved acknowledgement and gave them a cheery smile.

'When did you find out? Why didn't you tell me?' Daphne whispered anxiously.

'I only noticed this morning. It was sent last night,' Ibbie explained. 'I wanted to tell you but I knew you'd react like this.'

'When were you going to tell me?'

'I wasn't. Come on, Daphne. They won't give a hoot about my email. You said so yourself. I thought I'd let time pass and then, maybe months from now, let the cat out of the bag.'

'Let the cat out of the bag? You let him send the ruddy email.'

'Ssh! They'll think we're having an argument. Your face is like thunder.'

Effie approached them. 'Is everything okay?'

'Yes, fine,' Daphne lied, forcing a smile when she really felt like throttling her best friend.

Effie didn't believe them, but said no more about it, and asked instead for fabric to make curtains for the windows of her cottage. Her cottage was situated down at the shore, a few minutes walk from the main street.

Daphne cut the fabric for Effie while Ibbie poured a cup of tea.

The bee was quite busy. The ladies were seated around the sewing room, sipping tea and enjoying the cakes and sandwiches.

Ibbie sat down and began to unravel her knitting.

No one commented on the mess of her yarn, and all was fine for a few minutes until Daphne and Effie came through and joined them.

Florie smiled at Daphne and Ibbie. 'So, what have you pair been up to recently?' she asked cheerfully.

Ibbie gave Daphne a look of — well, should I tell them?

Daphne nodded and settled back in her chair to eat a chocolate éclair while Ibbie explained what happened.

Effie nearly choked on her tea. 'The cat sent the email to Hollywood?'

Ibbie shrugged. 'Technically, yes.'

Several of them burst out laughing.

Daphne relayed more details of what had happened that night in the shop.

'You can see our dilemma,' Ibbie concluded.

The sound of the sewing machines had ceased at the mention of Hollywood studios and heartthrob Shaw Starlight. The women listened, questioned, gasped and stared in disbelief.

'I don't expect a reply from them,' said Ibbie. 'I didn't intend to actually send the email.'

Effie rounded on her. 'Yes, but you wrote it, Ibbie. It didn't write itself.'

Something in Daphne appreciated Effie's no nonsense take on the issue.

'I did, but I'd been drinking wine and got carried away with thoughts of meeting Shaw Starlight. I mean, can you imagine? He's gorgeous. I know he wouldn't look twice at a wee squeef like me, but the thought that he might even see the email. . .' She sighed. 'I suppose I'm just an eejit.'

'What will you do if they want to come over here?' asked Florie.

Ibbie grinned. 'Come running to tell you lot to help us.'

'What are the chances of that happening?' said Effie.

Daphne calculated the odds. 'A million to one.'

'I don't think they'll even reply,' said Ibbie.

One of the ladies put her sewing down and looked at Ibbie. 'Did you tell them it was Scotland? Are you sure you emphasised that?'

Ibbie nodded and Daphne intervened. 'She'd actually pitched the email very well. And she'd certainly made it clear that the town was in Scotland.'

Effie laughed. 'You're as bad as Ibbie, and we thought she was a mischief maker.'

Ibbie looked wistful. 'It would be brilliant if they did read my message. I haven't sent many messages to Hollywood.'

Daphne's teacup clattered in her saucer. 'What do you mean many? Have you sent emails to Hollywood before?'

Ibbie's cheeks flushed. 'I might have, sort of. . . a while ago. I must've forgotten to mention it.'

Daphne glared at her.

'Did any of them reply to you?' Effie asked Ibbie.

'No. I never heard a peep. That's why I'm sure they won't answer me this time. The last couple of times was when I read adverts asking for film extras. It wasn't the same people. It was different companies.'

'You applied to work as a film extra?' Daphne sounded incredulous.

'Yes, twice. Those are the only emails I've sent and I never heard from anyone.'

One of the ladies smiled at Ibbie. 'There's nothing wrong in having daydreams about glamorous celebrities and all the glitter of Hollywood. I used to want to run off to London and be an actress in one of the theatres down there. I never did. I was only in my teens and as I got older I found all the happiness I needed right here.'

'You're just not settled in yourself, Ibbie. That rotten ex–boyfriend of yours has a lot to answer for,' said Effie.

They went on to discuss the reasons for Ibbie's obsession with Hollywood and came to the conclusion that it was Duncan's fault for breaking her heart.

Ibbie gave a resigned smile. 'Yes, you're probably right, but I'm over him now. I saw him last night at the chip shop and then he walked past my shop with his new girlfriend. She had a ring on her engagement finger.'

They'd heard the gossip.

'That was fast though,' said Effie. 'He's not long by dating you.'

Ibbie shrugged. 'Stuff him. Stuff the pair of them. I'm happy working in my wee shop.'

Daphne gave her a smile. 'And sending emails to Hollywood.'

'If it all goes awry,' said Effie, 'we'll blame John.'

Ibbie nodded firmly. 'Exactly. That cat is always up to something.'

'Just like his owner,' said Daphne.

They continued sewing and chatting for the remainder of the afternoon. Effie had brought dress patterns she'd designed herself to share with a few of the others. Various sizes were included.

'These are patterns from my days as a seamstress,' Effie explained. 'This pattern is for an easy to wear dress with sleeves, three–quarter length or full–length sleeves, and pockets. It skims the figure and is very flattering. You can wear it to go shopping, for work, or for a night out if you add a bit of jewellery and heels. I used to make it in soft jersey fabrics that wash and wear well. Daphne has suitable fabrics in the shop with a nice soft handle and drape. They're easy fabrics to sew and keep their shape. Lovely for dressmaking.'

'I'd love to sew a dress like that,' said one of the ladies. 'How many metres of fabric would I need?'

'Depending on the width of the fabric and the layout you choose, three or four metres would make you a dress,' Effie calculated. 'This pattern fits size twelve to eighteen, and I can help make adjustments if needed.'

The pattern was handed around and several women wanted to make one.

'I'm not confident using an overlocker to sew the seams, especially on a stretch jersey fabric,' said another member.

'I'll help you sew the seams,' Effie offered. 'And this is another pattern with a slightly different neckline, nice neat shoulders, but comfy fitting around the waist, again very wearable. It's handy having a dress or two like this in your wardrobe.' She handed the pattern around along with several other variations in size and style. 'Sometimes the old–fashioned patterns are the best.'

To speed things up for those who enjoyed sewing but weren't experienced in pattern cutting, Effie and Daphne cut several dresses ready to be stitched. The fabrics in the shop were popular and most chose plain colours in muted tones of navy, charcoal, burgundy and a very stylish old gold. Ibbie decided she wanted one in fuchsia pink and Daphne said she'd run it up for her in the sewing machine and adjust it to fit Ibbie's smaller frame.

The members helped each other, especially when it came to fitting in the sleeves and sewing the darts.

'When I've finished the dress, I'm going to embroider a flower or butterfly motif on it,' said one of the members.

'Embroidery adds a lovely personal touch to a dress or a top,' said Daphne.

16

'Does anyone have an embroidery pattern for a bumblebee or a butterfly?' asked June. 'I'd love to have a go at that. I've got embroidery threads I've hardly used.'

'I have patterns for bees, butterflies, moths, dragonflies and flowers,' said Daphne, 'and scraps of goldwork embroidery threads that you can use for adding a gilded element.'

'Thanks, Daphne,' said June.

She looked out lots of threads and patterns. 'These satin embroidery threads in sea blues, pinks and lilacs are wonderful for sewing seahorses, mermaids and fairies.'

June choose what she wanted, and the remainder of the patterns and threads were shared between the other women.

'I've also got these new colouring book fabrics,' said Daphne, showing them fat quarters she'd pre–cut for customers. The material was white cotton printed with black outline illustrations of flowers, bees and other pretty creatures. 'The idea is that you can colour in the designs using fabric markers or other suitable methods, but I find it's become popular with those who enjoy doing embroidery. It saves time having to transfer a design on to fabric as the outline is already there. It's perfect for embroidery. I've used it myself. I bought in designs that can be embroidered and used as quilt blocks, cushions, for framing and as clothing motifs.'

Daphne shared several off–cuts, but members also insisted in buying the fat quarters and threads for embroidering.

As the bee came to a close, a whole lot of sewing had been done, and the email predicament faded with the early evening light.

Daphne waved the last of the members off, many with the makings of a dress in their bags, and put the kettle on for a cuppa with Ibbie.

'I wish I could sew like you Daphne.' Ibbie admired the half finished fuchsia dress beside a sewing machine.

'And I wish I could knit like you.' Daphne sat down and worked on the dress while the kettle boiled. 'I'll work on this tonight and have it ready sometime tomorrow for you.'

'Thanks, Daph. I love the colour. I'll knit you a cardigan. I've got some really lovely soft yarn in.'

'You don't have to. I'm happy to make you a dress.'

'I want to. What colour would you like? The white is gorgeous, and white goes with everything. And pearl buttons.'

'Sounds lovely.'

Picturing what yarn she'd use, Ibbie made the tea while Daphne continued sewing, making huge progress with the dress.

Ibbie brought the tea through. 'Every time I come to the sewing bee I never need to cook dinner. I'm full of cake and sandwiches.'

Daphne finished sewing a seam and then sipped her tea. 'Want to sit outside in the garden and get some fresh air?'

Ibbie nodded and followed Daphne outside. They sat down at the garden table and drank their tea.

Daphne breathed in the scent of the flowers and gazed up at the sky. Bands of pink and lilac stretched across it like streaks of watercolour. 'I wonder if we're in for a storm? The flowers always smell extra potent when it's going to rain.'

Ibbie watched the sky change colour over the rooftops. 'I enjoy a summer rain storm.'

'Me too.'

'As long as it's bright and warm again in the morning,' said Ibbie.

'With everything washed clean and fresh.'

'Exactly.'

A low rumble sounded in the distance.

Daphne listened. 'Is that thunder?'

'Sounded like it.' Ibbie shivered. 'There's always an energy to a thunderstorm. It's like there's a sense of something — a change in things.'

Daphne nodded thoughtfully. The sky was darkening as they spoke, and the pink and lilac streaks were deepening to cerise and violet. And she sensed that yes, a change was coming up. She didn't know what it was, but perhaps this would be the last sewing bee before everything was different.

'Come on, let's go inside Ibbie before it buckets down.'

A few spits of rain hit off their faces as they walked across the garden and went inside.

Before closing the patio doors, Daphne gazed outside. Fast moving clouds swirled overhead, and a fresh sea breeze fluttered through the flowers.

'What are you doing tonight?' Ibbie asked.

'Updating my website with the latest fabrics. Dealing with online orders ready for posting in the morning, a bit of sewing and then getting some sleep. You?'

'Adding the new yarns to my website. Wrapping a few orders for delivery. Making a start on your cardigan, and watching a film on the telly.'

'Maybe we should think about organising a party night out like Effie suggested.'

'Would you be okay about going to Hew's hotel?'

'Yes, there's no awkwardness between us.'

'It's a pity you don't fancy him. Hew is okay. He's quite handsome.'

Daphne grinned. 'Florie certainly seems to think so.'

'You might change your mind about him when you see him again. He really fancies you.'

'Don't go interfering and matchmaking.'

Ibbie held up her hands. 'No meddling from me.'

The storm gathered pace as Ibbie helped Daphne tidy up the shop after the sewing bee. By the time they'd finished, it was pouring rain and Ibbie used an umbrella to run to her own shop.

Daphne went upstairs and worked on dealing with orders and updating her website. The rain battered off the living room window and made it feel extra cosy being inside, shielded from the storm.

The rain continued even as Daphne finally climbed into bed. She kept the curtains open, gazed out at the wild night, and snuggled under her patchwork quilt.

Daphne hurried to Nairna's bakery beside Ibbie's shop the next morning to buy rolls for breakfast. The main street was washed clean from all the rain, and bright sunshine was starting to burn through the pale overcast sky. The air was fresh and warm, and she wore a floral cotton dress with a cardigan.

'Morning, Daphne.' Nairna's greeting was always welcoming, even when the boyfriend she'd thought was going to ask her to marry him, left the town to marry someone else. She'd opened the bakery initially as a temporary pop–up shop, but it had been so successful she'd made it into a permanent venture. Although it was a modern bakery, Nairna's bread, cakes and scones had an old–fashioned quality to them and she used traditional recipes for her bakery items. Nairna was in her late twenties, but if anyone looked like they belonged to a bygone era it was her. There was something about her shiny auburn hair, hazel eyes, fresh complexion and slender build that suited wearing tea dresses and vintage aprons.

'Four morning rolls please, Nairna, and two vanilla cupcakes.'

Nairna bagged the items and as Daphne paid for them, Hew came into the shop looking dapper in his grey suit, white shirt and tie. Both Daphne and Hew were taken aback seeing each other. She hadn't seen him face–to–face for months. Even in a small town their paths rarely crossed.

He looked handsome, she thought. His light brown hair had gold strands where the sun had lightened it.

'Daphne,' he said, his pale blue eyes taking in everything about her.

She smiled, picked up her items, and left him to collect the special anniversary cake he'd ordered for his hotel from Nairna.

As she walked back to her shop she thought about him. Effie was right. Hew was overlooked by the women in town, but she didn't think he was the man for her.

She went upstairs to the kitchen, made tea, buttered two rolls and ate them while still pondering about Hew and getting her shop ready for opening. The flowers in her garden had taken a battering in the storm and she cut a bunch of them and put them in a vase in the shop window. The fragrance of the sweet peas and lily of the valley filled the air.

Mondays were often busy for postal deliveries, and a courier arrived to pick up the parcels of fabric and dresses for her online customers.

Ibbie dropped in to show her the white yarn she'd chosen for the cardigan, and grab a cupcake, before running back to attend to her own customers. The morning whizzed past and by late afternoon Daphne realised she'd hardly stopped all day. She'd even finished sewing Ibbie dress. Except for a fitting to decide on the length of the hem, the dress was ready.

Daphne planned to pop into Ibbie's shop around closing time at five o'clock, get her to try the dress on and quickly sew the hem.

But Daphne's plan didn't quite go as expected.

CHAPTER THREE

Hollywood Los Angeles

'Who are these people?' the director asked his assistant.

'They're Scottish.'

'Scottish?'

'Eh, yes. They're based in Scotland.'

'In Scotland? Don't they understand the brief?'

'They do, however. . .' Travis glanced at the name on the email, 'Ibbie says their main street is a hive of business and could, on a dark rainy night, pass for Los Angeles.'

Jefersen frowned. 'Rainy night?'

'It's Scotland.'

'Ah, yes.'

'But she says it would add to the dramatic atmosphere.'

'I suppose so. . .' Jefersen squinted at the map. 'Where exactly did you say they're located? Is it near the city of Glasgow?'

'Ibbie says it's further down, on the West Coast. There's the bay. She's highlighted it and emphasises that it's a sweeping bay with a sparkly sea.'

'It looks beautiful — and does it have the airport we're looking for?'

'The airport is only a short drive away. And there's an airport in Glasgow which isn't that far.'

Jefersen nodded, his expression impressed. 'I'm starting to like this location. Can we see it from another view on the map?'

Travis pulled the image up on the screen but the town of Seaheath seemed to disappear.

'Where did it go?'

'She says it's down there somewhere. You just can't see it because a cloud was going over when the view was snapped.'

Jefersen nodded thoughtfully. He was tall, fit, long–limbed, with blond hair, mid–thirties, and had sea green eyes that seemed fascinated with the idea of filming in Scotland.

'They're keen, they're cheap and we could take advantage of the location,' said Travis. He was similar in build, early thirties, with

21

well–cut dark hair and vivid blue eyes. 'The press would take an interest if we filmed there and managed to create L.A. in a little town like this in Scotland.'

'They would, wouldn't they. . .'

'If we film these scenes of the movie in Canada the press won't be interested. We usually film there. But no one would film part of a movie of this magnitude in a niche in Scotland that's so small it's hardly a pinprick on the map.'

Jefersen looked around the office that had a view overlooking Hollywood. 'Where's Shaw? He was supposed to be here.'

'He's having his highlights done.'

Jefersen studied the photographs of Ibbie and Daphne in their swimsuits. 'The women look lovely. Feisty, but very attractive.'

'That one is Ibbie. The impish one with the red hair and polka dot swimsuit attempting the splits. The blonde eating an ice cream cone is Daphne. They own shops in the town.'

'Yeah, maybe this would work. . . Scotland. . . I always wanted to vacation there.'

Ibbie's laptop was open on the knitting shop counter. She stared at it in disbelief as Daphne walked in carrying the dress just before five o'clock.

'Oh, shite.'

'What's wrong?' said Daphne.

Ibbie pointed to the email reply. Her hand shook. 'They've said yes. They're coming over here to film.'

Daphne glanced at the email. 'Shite. What are we going to do?'

'Get our highlights done before they get here.'

Daphne looked at the laptop screen. 'What else does it say in the email?'

Ibbie opened the first attachment. 'Jeez, there's a ream of stuff.'

'What's the gist?'

'The director has authorised a production unit to go on location to Scotland for two weeks. He's listed the dates. They've alerted their London office who have contacted a studio and film crew in the Midlands and they're going to send people up to get the ball rolling. They'll need accommodation and have asked if we can recommend any hotels or bed and breakfasts available.'

'There's Hew's hotel. He'd be handy. We could ask him.'

Ibbie skimmed the details. 'It says Jefersen, the director, wants to speak to me and will call me at 9:00 a.m. Los Angeles time. When will that be in our time?'

'I'm not sure if they're eight hours ahead of the UK or behind us.'

Ibbie typed a search into the laptop. 'They're eight hours behind us, so if he was going to phone me it would be round about—'

The phone rang.

'Now!' shrieked Ibbie.

'Calm down, calm down and answer it. Try to sound casual.'

Ibbie trembled as she said, 'Hello.'

'Hi, this is Jefersen. I'm calling from Hollywood. Can I speak to Ibbie?' He had a rich, smooth, American accent.

Daphne watched the colour drain from Ibbie's already pale features. Ibbie's mouth opened but no words came out.

Daphne grabbed the phone as Ibbie's legs buckled and she slowly folded down into the wool display.

John thought Ibbie was playing and joined in the fun, bounding over and padding across the wool and on to Ibbie's lap.

Daphne took a deep breath, clicked the call to speakerphone so Ibbie could hear, and tried to sound like her friend's lighter tone. 'Hi, this is Ibbie.'

'Did you get my email?'

'Yes, thanks for phoning, and it's great that you want to film here.'

'My assistant, Travis, will be in touch, and the guy who is in charge of the UK movie crew. He'll call tomorrow, your time, to give you details of what we need and send the contracts up.'

'Contracts?'

'Yeah. Have your people look over them. There are standard fees we pay for location hire. We'll also hire a few locals for background.'

'That's great.'

Ibbie started to regain control after her mild fainting, but John was concerned and began meowing at her.

'Is that a cat I hear?' he asked.

'Erm, yes.'

'Is he your cat? Is he domesticated?'

'He is. To both questions.'

23

'Is he a good looking cat?'

Daphne glanced at the unkempt fur ball. 'John is. . . he's very. . . affectionate.'

'The cat's called John? An unusual name for a cat.'

'It's actually quite a popular name for cats here.'

'Hey, it's a solid name. So, he's cute?'

John meowed again.

The director laughed. 'The reason I'm asking is, we have a cat in the movie. Our leading lady, Tiara Timberlane, owns a cat in the storyline, and if you have a well behaved cat, it would save us having to bring one up from England or hire a cat trainer.'

'I'm sure you could use John. He's. . . as I said. . . very affectionate.'

'What colour is he?'

'He's sort of brownish, greyish.'

'Adaptable.'

'Yes.' Daphne hoped she'd given him a fair description.

'I'll have Travis send a contract for him. The usual rate. Is that okay?'

'Yes, yes.'

'Oh and email a photograph of John to me. We'll start circulating him as part of the publicity.'

'Publicity?'

'Yeah, we're highlighting the fact that we're filming in Scotland. The UK press will no doubt be in touch with you soon.'

Daphne tried to suppress the anxiety in her voice. 'Okay.'

'Great talking to you, Ibbie, and we'll speak again soon. And remember to send a cute pic of the cat. Bye.'

And he was gone.

Daphne and Ibbie stared at each other and then at the cat.

'We love him,' said Ibbie, 'but John looks hellish.'

'We can tart him up. Get his grooming brush. I'll see what I can do to tidy up his tail.'

John was in his element, being pampered, having his fur brushed.

'I'll forward this email from the director to my aunt and give her a quick call.' Ibbie checked the time. 'She'll still be working in the council office.'

Daphne carefully brushed the tangles from the cat's tail while Ibbie phoned her aunt who squealed with glee at the prospect of the filming.

'Tell your boss to read the bumph asap,' Ibbie told her aunt. 'I know, it's so exciting.' She paused. 'Yes, you should get your hair done. Daphne's tarting up John for his photos. All right. I have to go and help Daph.'

'We'll take a photo of him in the garden while there's still some sunlight.' Daphne picked John up and carried him outside. He purred all the way.

'I'll get my phone. I use it for all my photos.' Ibbie dashed to get it and then hurried out.

Daphne put John beside the sweet peas and fluffed up his fur. 'We can use the flowers to help disguise him.'

Ibbie crouched down and focused on John. She was used to taking photographs of her knitting for her website and had a small table set up in the back of the shop with a couple of spotlights. But for the outdoor pics, she relied on the natural light and took a couple using the flash. John purred loudly throughout the photo–shoot, loving being fluffed and fussed over.

Ibbie looked at one of the photos. John was sniffing the flowers and she'd snapped him at a flattering angle. 'I think this one is a winner.'

Daphne glanced at it. 'Yes. Great one.'

'Do you think we should take one of him smiling?'

Daphne frowned at her. 'Smiling?'

'If I mention his favourite s–a–r–d–i–n–e cat food,' she said, spelling it out, 'he does that thing where he shows his top teeth as if he's grinning. He loves it.'

'Do you have any of it?'

'I've got a tin upstairs. I'll run up and get it.'

Daphne took several other photos of John in different parts of the garden, including an action shot as he jumped up trying to catch a wasp. He missed, but the mid–leap photo made him look playful.

Ibbie came rushing back with the tin of cat food. 'Get ready to snap his wee face.'

Daphne lined up the shot. 'Go for it.'

'Sardine din–dins, John,' Ibbie repeated a few times, though once was enough to create a reaction.

'Got him! What a smile, or grin or grimace.' Daphne flicked through the photos. 'One of these will work.'

Then they took him inside and set him up beside the knitting, angling the spotlights to highlight him.

'We'll give him his dinner in a minute,' said Ibbie, brushing his fur until it was as smooth as possible, then fluffing it for a different look. 'We won't know what pics are best until I've uploaded them on to the laptop.'

While Ibbie scanned the photos, Daphne fed John. They left him munching his favourite dinner in the back of the shop while they made their selection.

'That one. It's a definite.' Daphne pointed to one where John was smiling directly into the camera. 'Some of his teeth are wonky, but it gives him character.'

'I bet they've never seen a cat smile like that before,' Ibbie said proudly.

Daphne didn't doubt it.

'And it's a toss up between the one where he's sniffing the flowers and the action–pouncing one.' Daphne flicked between the two and couldn't decide.

'I also like this one of his cheeky face peering through the flowers,' said Ibbie. 'It's the closest to cute I've ever seen him.'

Daphne agreed. 'Maybe we can send a selection and let them pick what ones they want to use for the publicity.'

And that's what they did. Ibbie emailed the images to the director, not expecting he'd reply quickly confirming he'd received them and that John was fantastic.

Ibbie plonked herself down beside the knitting display. 'I don't know about you, but I'm knackered. I think it's all the excitement. I haven't taken it in, that they're really coming over here, and yet. . . the thought of getting to meet Shaw Starlight is amazing.'

'We probably need to sleep on it.'

'And then panic.'

Daphne laughed. 'I can't believe you've actually convinced them to film here.'

'The director sounded luscious, didn't he?'

'He did. He's got a sexy voice.'

Ibbie got up quickly and typed at her laptop. 'Let's see what he looks like.' She typed his name into a search.

Daphne peered over her shoulder as they found recent images of Jefersen.

They looked at each other and nodded.

'Wow,' said Daphne.

'Wow indeed,' Ibbie agreed. 'He's a blond hottie.'

Daphne looked at one of the pictures with the names captioned. 'There's his assistant, Travis, standing beside him at a film event.

'Oh, I like Travis,' Ibbie enthused. 'Very suave and sexy.'

'They're both really handsome, Ibbie.'

'And then there's Shaw Starlight. I don't think my heart will calm down for a month.'

The phone rang.

'Jeez, it's Hollywood again. It says it's an international call. It must be the director.'

'Pick it up, Ibbie. Put it on speakerphone so I can hear. Deep breath and go for it.'

Ibbie took a calming breath. 'Hello, this is Ibbie.'

'Hi, Ibbie. I'm Travis. I believe Jefersen told you I'd call.'

Daphne nodded at Ibbie, waved her arms, encouraging her to sound calm but upbeat.

'Yes, he did. I've sent the information that was attached in the email to the local council. They're delighted you're coming over and are reading the bumph.'

Travis laughed.

'What I mean is,' Ibbie tried to correct herself.

'I know what you mean,' he said. His American accent and tone was slightly lighter than the director's voice. 'I've already contacted the UK crew. They're used to working at short notice, so they're driving up from the midlands overnight and should be with you in the morning. If you have any local hotel or accommodation suggestions, let me know.'

'There's a hotel. We know the owner, Hew. It's a lovely, traditional hotel. We haven't spoken to Hew yet, but he fancies Daphne so he'll bend over backwards to accommodate you if she asks him.'

Daphne could've strangled her friend.

Ibbie realised her mistake, but it was too late to undo it.

'I'm sure quite a few guys admire you and Daphne. You're both very attractive.'

27

'Oh, well. . .' Ibbie faltered, 'we're flattered as hell.'
He laughed again.

'I love your accent,' he said. 'Are you going to be taking part in the movie as one of the background people?'

'Definitely. So is Daphne.' She mouthed to Daphne who had no intention of being in the film. *Phone Hew.*

'Great. It'll be fun,' said Travis. 'We've filmed most of the movie. These are some of the final scenes, but Jefersen is known for his artistic adaptability. He wrote the script as well as being the director, so this gives him amazing creative control.'

'Sounds fascinating.'

While Ibbie and Travis continued to chat, Daphne phoned Hew at the hotel and explained the dilemma. She was impressed by how calm and efficient he was in handling the situation, promising them accommodation and the use of his hotel car park for the film crew to park their vehicles when they arrived.

'Thanks, Hew,' Daphne whispered. 'I'll pass your number on to Travis.'

Daphne gave Ibbie the thumbs up and scribbled Hew's phone number down for her to tell Travis.

'Daphne's just contacted Hew and he's happy to help. I'll give you his number.'

John padded through having finished his dinner. He entwined himself around Ibbie's ankles looking for attention and meowed loudly when she wasn't quick enough to clap him.

Daphne picked him up and he snuggled into her.

'Was that John?' asked Travis.

'Yes. He's a talkative one and likes attention,' Ibbie explained.

'I saw the photos of him. Jefersen says he's ideal. Tiara was promised a white cat for the jeopardy scenes, but he thinks John's look is far more. . .daring. This will work better with the stunts.'

Ibbie sounded concerned. 'John will have to do stunts?'

'No, no. . . well. . .nothing dangerous. He just has to sit on Tiara's lap for a couple of interior close–ups when she's kidnapped in the car. Shaw rescues her of course, but Jefersen has it all figured out, so no worries. And the guys in England are bringing up a sports car for Shaw to drive in the chase scene. The stunt fight coordinator and three of his guys are bringing the car up and they'll organise the action.'

'Sounds like it's all under control.'

'It is. We've done things like this lots of times. Adaptability is necessary in our business. As you can appreciate, being a businesswoman, you often have to go with the flow, especially as we're on a tight time schedule with this movie and already slamming hard against the clock. But it'll be fine. Always is. Chaos and creativity are part of the game.'

'Chaos and creativity defines my knitting shop perfectly. Sometimes when I've caught up with the online yarn orders and think I can relax at night and watch a film or a show on the telly, I'll get a glut of enquires and new orders after my dinner and have to spend the evening packing the parcels ready for the courier to collect in the morning. Sometimes it seems unending.'

'That's what happens when you work for yourself, but I reckon it's worth it.'

'Do you work for Jefersen or the studio?'

'For Jefersen. I've made a couple of shorts and commercials. I'm hoping to step into feature film directing soon full–time.'

'Become another Jefersen?'

'Yeah. He's so generous in sharing his knowledge. We work well together, but we're both from movie families. Jefersen's father was a major producer and director, so it was natural he'd follow his dad's lead. And my mom was a wardrobe assistant and now also works on the production side of things. My dad is a cameraman and I'm interested in becoming a director. I have a couple of projects lined up after we finish this movie.'

'It sounds amazing. It must be great working in Hollywood,' Ibbie enthused.

'It is. I love it. You ever been over here?'

'No, not yet.'

'You should come over for the L.A. premiere and bring Daphne. You'd both have a great time.'

Ibbie opened her mouth wide and gawped excitedly at Daphne. John had fallen asleep on Daphne's lap and she hoped Travis couldn't hear his guttural snoring.

'When will the film be released?' Ibbie asked Travis.

'It's scheduled for a summer release next year, but Jefersen has been in the editing suite working on it like crazy, so he's got a lot in the can, and wants to push for an earlier release. That's why it's so important to get things moving with you guys as soon as possible. We're working on the pre–publicity already, and if the shoot in Scotland works well, Jefersen plans to cut an early trailer for general release to get some buzz on it. This will help with distribution, which is what Jef hopes to achieve with the cat angle — plenty of publicity on your side of the pond and in the US.'

Ibbie wasn't sure her brain could take any more information or excitement. She handed the phone to Daphne and fanned herself, looking flushed and flustered.

'Daphne wants to talk to you.'

Unable to refuse, Daphne spoke to Travis. 'If you call Hew, he'll organise the film crew's accommodation at his hotel.'

'I'll do that. I'm flying over with Jefersen, Shaw and Tiara sometime tomorrow hopefully, so we should be with you on Wednesday. I'll talk to your hotel guy, Hew, about booking our rooms.'

'Yes, he'll sort you out.'

'I believe you own a dress shop in town.'

'I do. I'm a dressmaker and I sell fabric too.'

'We're looking forward to meeting you.'

They finished the call so that Travis could phone Hew.

Daphne looked as flushed as Ibbie. 'I didn't know what else to say to him. Jeez, he's got such a lovely voice too.'

Ibbie sighed. 'What are we going to do now?'

'Phone the sewing bee ladies and tell them what's happened.'

CHAPTER FOUR

Tea Dresses and Quilts

'I'm on my way to your shop, Daphne,' said Effie. 'We need a plan of action. I'll round up the girls if you can rustle up the tea.'

'I'll put the kettle on,' Daphne told her.

Ibbie followed Daphne into her shop and they both set up cups for the tea while the kettle boiled. Several members arrived, all a fluster, along with Ethel and Ivy.

'Is it true?' said June. 'Are they really arriving tomorrow?'

'The crew from England are,' Daphne explained while they helped themselves to tea and biscuits. 'The director, his assistant and the stars should arrive on Wednesday.'

'Where are we going to put them all?' asked Florie. 'Hew's hotel has a number of rooms, but what if he doesn't have enough?'

'Hew has Ivy and me on a short list of cottage accommodation, like bed and breakfast, for when there's an overspill. You know how busy he gets during the golf events,' said Effie.

The women nodded.

'So you could potentially have Shaw Starlight staying in your cottage Ethel?' said Ibbie.

'No, he'll get the star treatment of the top room in the hotel,' Ethel told her. 'The Hollywood actors will get the cream of the accommodation along with the director and his assistant.'

'What did they sound like when you spoke to them?' June asked Ibbie.

Ibbie grinned. 'They've got sexy voices and sounded very friendly. And they're handsome, really luscious.'

The women's interest increased.

'We looked up their profiles and pictures online,' Ibbie explained.

Daphne accessed the pictures and information on her laptop and set it up on the shop counter. The women crowded round to study them.

'That's Jefersen the director,' said Daphne.

'He's younger than I imagined,' Effie commented. 'Very handsome. I love men with thick blond hair.'

They went on to study Travis.

'He's gorgeous too,' said June.

Ibbie nodded. 'I tried to get a close–up of Travis. I think he's got beautiful blue eyes, and although if he lived here he'd be quite pale, he suits having a light tan.'

'He's got nice dark hair,' one of them said.

'I wonder if they're married?' said Ivy.

Florie looked at her gran. 'Don't you start putting wild ideas into our heads. It's crazy enough that they'll be here on Wednesday, never mind dreaming about romancing them.'

'Nothing wrong with dreaming about handsome men, Florie,' Ivy told her.

Effie's phone rang. 'It's Hew. I wonder if there's something up?' She answered it. 'Hello, Hew. Yes, I'm with the girls at Daphne's shop.' She listened to what he had to say. 'Yes, I could, and Ivy's got two spare rooms in her cottage too. We could put four of them up. All right. Yes, Hew. I will. Speak to you later.' She hung up.

'What's happening?' said Daphne.

'Hew needs extra rooms, so he's commandeered my cottage and Ivy's cottage for the stunt fight coordinator and his three stuntmen. They're happy to stay down the shore as it'll allow them to do their daily training and run along the sand.'

Ivy was aghast. 'Stuntmen? How many am I going to have living with me?'

'We'll have two each, Ivy.'

The women burst out laughing.

'I'll have to get their rooms ready,' said Ivy.

Florie and others offered to help them. 'But your cottages are always neat as pins,' said Florie, 'especially yours, gran.'

Ivy smiled. 'I pride myself in keeping a tidy house. You never know when someone is going to drop in, though never in my wildest dreams would I have thought I'd be looking after two Hollywood stuntmen.'

Florie giggled. 'Nothing wrong with dreaming about handsome men though, eh, gran?'

Ivy laughed, then she said, 'I wonder if they need a special diet?'

'Nonsense,' Ethel said emphatically. 'They'll eat good old–fashioned home cooking and like it. I did my shopping today, so my fridge is well–stocked. I probably only need more milk and eggs.'

Ivy spoke about her quilts. 'Thankfully, I've finished sewing two new quilts. One of them is a traditional design and the other is the one I've been stitching at the sewing bee — with lily of the valley embroidery.'

'We may have to reschedule the Wednesday night sewing bee,' said Daphne.

Effie guffawed. 'Reschedule the bee? We're going to be buzzing around these film people until they leave. I'm so excited.'

The women headed down to the cottages on the shore which were a couple of minutes walk from the main street, leaving Daphne and Ibbie to continue with their plans.

'What are our plans?' asked Ibbie, 'apart from getting our hair done?'

'We won't have time to go to the hairdresser, so wash and blow dry your hair in the morning. I'll do the same. We need to make sure our shops look extra tidy. Decide what to wear if we need to meet the film crew tomorrow. I think they'll expect to talk to your aunt and her boss from the council, so update her on what's happening.'

Ibbie nodded.

'Apart from that,' Daphne continued, 'try to get some sleep so we don't look knackered tomorrow.'

'At least Shaw Starlight, Jefersen and Travis won't arrive until the following day, so that gives us a bit of time to draw breath.'

'We won't have much time for that.'

Ibbie's phone rang. 'I don't recognise the number.' She answered it and mouthed to Daphne that it was a newspaper journalist. 'I'll let you speak to Daphne about the film. She's the verbose one.' She thrust the phone into Daphne's unsure grasp.

Daphne did her utmost to explain the details to the journalist. He seemed particularly interested in the cat.

'John has secured a part in the film,' said Daphne. 'We've sent photos of him to the director in Hollywood and—' she paused as he interrupted. 'Yes, we'll email a copy of the photos to you at the paper. What's your email?'

Daphne told him she'd send the photos of John along with the pictures Ibbie had sent in her original pitch. Daphne tried to persuade the journalist to use other pictures of them instead of the swimsuit photos, but he wanted the ones that the director saw and liked enough to phone them.

'What made your friend, Ibbie, think that your little town in Scotland could look like Los Angeles?' he asked.

'She thought it was feasible, and the director seems to think he can film here.'

'Could I speak to Ibbie to get a direct quote from her?'

Daphne handed the phone to Ibbie.

'When you wrote the email, did you ever think the director would accept your suggestion?'

'Not in a million years,' Ibbie told him. 'I wrote it, then showed it to Daphne and we decided not to send it because our wee town is nothing like Los Angeles.'

'What made you change your mind?'

'It was sent by accident. John stepped on the laptop and his paw pressed the send button.'

Daphne gasped and glared at Ibbie.

'Your cat sent the email? Is that correct?' There was laughter in the journalist's voice.

Daphne shook her head at Ibbie, but as she'd already let slip about what happened she couldn't undo it.

'Did John send the email to Hollywood, Ibbie?' he prompted her.

'Yes,' she admitted. 'He did. But you don't need to print that in the paper, do you?'

'It's a great story. Readers will love it,' he assured her.

After the call, Daphne and Ibbie wondered what to do.

Daphne tried to sound reasonable. 'He might not mention that John is responsible. You never know what journalists will put in the paper.'

'I'm sorry, I'm tired and overexcited and I've never spoken to a newspaper journalist before. I blab too much. Do you think we should tell Travis?'

'Maybe we should wait to see if the story is in the paper.'

Ibbie nodded. 'I need a cup of tea.'

Daphne boiled the kettle.

They had tea and helped each other tidy up their shops. John had fallen asleep in his cat basket so they let him snooze while they worked around him.

Daphne finished sewing the hem on Ibbie's new dress so she could wear it to meet Shaw Starlight.

Ibbie's aunt and the council boss phoned several times, confirming details of the paperwork and things they planned to discuss with the film crew at Hew's hotel when they arrived. The boss had even phoned Travis to let him know how pleased they were about the film and that Hew was organising a welcoming party when they arrived from America.

So all was well.

Ibbie flopped down on a chair in her shop. 'I'm puggled.'

'Me too. I'm going to get some sleep.'

'I don't think I'll sleep for excitement. It's worse than Christmas, and you know how hyper I am then.'

Daphne smiled and looked out the shop window at the activity in the main street. 'You won't be the only one. Have you seen the chaos outside?'

Ibbie got up and they both peered out the front door. Businesses that were usually closed for the night were a hive of activity. Shops were all lit up, busy with people running around, washing their shop windows, organising their displays, helping each other. Two men were mowing the lawn in front of a town building and flowers were being planted in window boxes.

People were up ladders giving shop fascias a fresh lick of paint, signs were cleaned and twinkle lights were being strung up on the lamp posts all along the main street.

'It's bedlam out there,' said Ibbie.

Daphne started to laugh.

'What's so funny? We're the cause of all this kerfuffle.'

'Look at the street, *look* at it. It's jumping with people faffing around, and it's all lit up.'

Ibbie eyes widened. 'It's looking a lot more like Los Angeles.'

And then they both laughed.

Daphne picked up her bag. 'See you in the morning, troublemaker.'

Ibbie smiled. 'Who me?'

Daphne went next door and got ready for bed. She peeked out the bedroom window at the street. It was still busy with people. The pubs and bar restaurant were doing a great trade and she could sense the excitement from everyone.

She saw Effie coming out of the grocery shop wheeling a trolley. The stuntmen were in for some tasty home cooking. And there was Florie and Ivy — and Hew. He'd been heading into the shop but Florie had waylaid him and her body language showed she was politely flirting with him. She didn't feel jealous of Florie. After all, she wasn't interested in Hew, even though he did look handsome in his suit.

She went to bed wondering what Jefersen, Travis and the film stars would be like in real life. She'd never met any actors and certainly not Hollywood stars. Jefersen sounded nice on the phone, so did Travis, but she'd always liked men with blond hair. Not that she thought there was any chance of romance with a film director. He probably had a girlfriend. Men like him were rarely single and available. She'd been tempted to look him up online and his profile said he wasn't married. But anyway. . . she'd have enough to deal with when Ibbie met Shaw Starlight. What a fiasco that was going to be. Shaw had never married and there had been a rumour that he'd dated Tiara Timberlane, but she'd totally denied it. Totally.

Tiara was very glamorous — a gorgeous brunette in her late twenties with lovely alabaster skin and blue eyes. Daphne had seen a couple of her films and enjoyed them. One was an action adventure and the other was a romantic drama. If this new film was anything like them, she'd enjoy it too. She hoped Tiara would be happy with John rather than the white cat she'd been promised.

With her mind ticking over everything, she finally fell asleep, only to be woken up a short time later by two customers knocking on her shop door wanting to buy the tea dresses in the window.

Daphne padded down in her slippers and pyjamas and sold them the dresses, both traditional tea dresses like the one she planned to wear in the morning. She flicked the lights off and went back upstairs, made a cup of tea and climbed into bed.

And then her phone rang. It was Ibbie.

'Are you asleep, Daphne?'

'Yes.'

'I can't sleep — and I saw you had customers in your shop at this time of night. The town's gone crazy busy. John's snoring in his basket. I'm going to get up early and run to the newsagents in the morning for the paper to see if he's in it, and if we're in it. I've never been in a newspaper before and I don't think you have either.'

36

Daphne sat in bed sipping her tea while Ibbie continued. 'I've made a start on your cardigan. I couldn't concentrate on anything else, so I've knitted the rib and part of the back. It's beautiful yarn and coming up a treat. And I've pressed the seams on my new dress. You've made a lovely job of it, Daph. I suppose you'll wear one of your pretty floral print tea dresses. You suit them so well. Oh and I've run out of my gloss enhancing shampoo so I wondered if I could borrow a dollop of yours? I'll pick it up on my way back from the newsagents.' She took a deep breath. 'So we'll need to stop chatting and get some sleep. See you in the morning. Night.'

Daphne put her empty cup down on the bedside table and settled down again, listening to the sounds of happy chaos outside until she fell asleep.

CHAPTER FIVE

Bumblebee Embroidery

Early the next morning the film crew arrived in several large vans, parked in the hotel car park, and were welcomed by Hew and his staff. Rooms were allocated and everyone was given breakfast and settled into their accommodation.

Hew phoned Ibbie. 'The film crew have arrived. They're a cheerful lot and I think they'll be pleasant to work with. I tried to phone Daphne but she didn't pick up. I left a message for her.'

Ibbie hurried along the street carrying copies of the newspaper. The sun shone in a bright blue sky making the main street feel summery. The shop windows reflected the sunlight and everything looked freshly laundered. 'That's great. I'm on my way to Daphne's shop with the daily newspaper. Have you seen it?'

'No, I haven't had a chance. Which one is it?'

Ibbie told him, and about the interview. 'I've barely slept and haven't had breakfast so I don't know whether to jump for glee or run for the hills. My stomach's flipping like a butter churn. The headline is a corker.'

'Hold on, I've got the paper at the reception desk.'

She heard him hurrying through from his office to read it. She gave him a moment to digest the story.

'Oh my goodness!'

'What do you think, Hew? Should I swap my strappy sandals for trainers?'

She heard the newspaper rustling. 'There are photos of you and Daphne in swimsuits. She's eating an ice cream cone. She looks lovely, obviously, but what were you thinking giving the press pictures of the two of you half naked?'

'We're not. We're down the shore on a sunny day in our swimwear.'

'And why are you attempting to do the splits?'

One of Hew's staff came rushing over with a copy of the paper, not knowing he was on the phone to Ibbie. 'Have you seen the headline news? They're saying the cat sent the email to Hollywood. And what is that daft Ibbie doing the splits for?'

'Yes, thanks, Barra. I'm talking to Ibbie right now.'

Barra held up his hands and disappeared back to where he'd come from.

'What do you think Daphne's reaction will be to the headline?' Ibbie asked tentatively.

'*Cat emails Hollywood and lands film role.*' Hew tried not to laugh. 'Better get your running shoes on, Ibbie.'

'Thanks a million,' she said huffily. She could still hear him laughing as she clicked the phone off and steeled herself to wake up Daphne.

Daphne was up and had just jumped out of the shower when Ibbie knocked on her shop door. She came downstairs in her robe and opened it, her face excited and concerned when she saw that Ibbie was armed with a pile of newspapers.

Ibbie dumped them down on the counter and shook her arms. 'I bought extra copies in case our customers or the sewing bee women want to read the story.'

Daphne's hair was still damp as she grabbed a copy.

'Page ten,' Ibbie said helpfully.

'You don't sound thrilled. Is it vile? Is it slanted? Is it a load of codswallop?' Then she saw the headline, and froze.

Ibbie couldn't stand the pause. 'Well, what do you think? Are we in the shit?'

'I don't know. I mean, wow — look at the size of those photos. They've really printed them bigger than I'd hoped. You can see every crevice in your swimsuit. And I mean *every* crevice.'

'But the headline? Is it a good thing or rotten?'

Daphne reread it. 'It's certainly an attention grabber. Jefersen and Travis wanted publicity and they've got it with bells on.'

Ibbie leaned in and pointed at the two pictures of John. They'd chosen the one of him smiling for the main photo and a smaller one of him peeking through the flowers. 'John looks great, doesn't he?'

'He does.' She sighed heavily. 'I think I need a cuppa.'

'I'll put the kettle on, and I've got rolls for our breakfast. We'll think better with some grub in us.'

They hurried upstairs.

'Take my shampoo if you need it,' said Daphne.

'Thanks.' Ibbie started to make breakfast. 'Hew phoned,' she called to Daphne who was busy getting dressed. She'd chosen a cream tea dress with a rose print. Ibbie wore cropped trousers and a vibrant multicoloured top that suited her neat figure. 'He said the film crew have arrived.' She explained everything he'd said.

Daphne came through to the kitchen and sipped her tea. 'If Hew, your aunt and her boss are dealing with them, we don't actually have to do anything.'

'That's right. We should keep busy in our shops and wait until Travis contacts us.'

'I have a few online orders I need to deal with.'

'Me too,' said Ibbie. 'And I'll wash my hair.'

For the remainder of the morning they worked in their shops, occasionally being interrupted by phone calls from Ibbie's aunt updating them on handling the film crew, and people waving in at them and laughing about the story in the newspaper.

Effie came scurrying in to talk to them in the knitting shop after lunch. Her cheeks were flushed and she kept gushing about the stuntmen in her cottage.

'Oh they're gorgeous, very fit and strong. I've got the stunt fight coordinator and one of his men — an expert kickboxer. I was making him scrambled eggs and he was stretching his leg all the way up the kitchen door, limbering up.' She flushed further. 'I tell you, I'd scramble that man's eggs for him any day.'

'So you're okay having them at the cottage?' said Daphne.

'Definitely. They're very polite and helpful. The stunt coordinator has moved my garden slabs for me. I'd left them leaning against the back wall since the autumn. He was outside doing bare–chested press–ups on the lawn and asked me if I wanted them laid. I told him I'd left them lying because they were too heavy for me to move and hadn't gotten around to hiring someone to help put them along the edge of the cottage, so he lifted them up as if they were wafers and put them down for me.'

'What about Ivy?' asked Daphne. 'Is she coping?'

'She's as delighted as me. She's got the tall, blond one who is Shaw Starlight's stunt double. And the other man is a stunt driver. The sports car that's going to be used in the film is parked outside her cottage.'

'Does Shaw's stunt double look like him?' Ibbie asked. 'Is he as handsome?'

'He's similar but obviously Shaw Starlight is chocolate box handsome. His double is a bit more rugged around the jaw. You should come down and meet them.'

Ibbie nodded enthusiastically. 'Yes, we will. You can introduce us.'

'Huh! I won't need to. They've seen your pictures in the paper and so has everyone else in the town. The pair of you are infamous.'

Daphne looked concerned.

Effie held up her shopping bag. 'I popped to the grocery shop for more flour to make puff pastry. I've promised to cook them steak pie, so I'd better get going. They're away for a run along the shore.'

And off she went, waving excitedly.

Ibbie picked up John and hugged him close. 'I'm getting more nervous as the day goes on.'

Daphne tried to sound confident. 'If Effie and Ivy can handle things, so can we.'

Ibbie put John in his basket. 'You're right, but. . .we're infamous, they're not.'

'We'll just have to brazen it out.'

The welcoming party Hew planned for the director and others from Hollywood was being organised, and he'd ordered a special cake for them from Nairna. Various local businesses were involved in helping get everything prepared for when they arrived on the Wednesday.

Ibbie sat down in Daphne's shop at closing time.

'It's been a busy day. I'm glad because I wish it was tomorrow and we were getting ready for the party and to meet Shaw Starlight.'

Daphne gazed out the window at the early evening sky. 'They'll be on the plane by now.'

Ibbie gazed out too. 'I've a feeling about these people, especially Travis and Jefersen.'

Daphne sensed it too. 'I know what you mean. It's as if nothing is ever going to be the same again.'

As the town buzzed with the arrival of the UK film crew, and some of the shops and the bar restaurant were commandeered by them, Daphne and Ibbie parcelled up their online orders ready for the morning courier and then caught up on the sleep they'd missed the previous night.

Another busy day beckoned in their shops and Daphne had extra enquires about her dresses and fabric from people who'd seen her in the newspaper. Ibbie noticed an increase in trade too.

As the excitement built for the arrival of the Hollywood stars, Daphne and Ibbie were kept busy with customers, emails and phone calls. Daphne also had increased sales of her embroidery items including the bumblebee embroidery patterns, butterfly designs, floral appliqué and embroidery thread. She often embroidered the dresses she made, adding a little bumblebee, butterfly or flower in threads that toned in with the fabric.

The sewing bee evening was postponed in favour of attending the film party and all members were planning to go for a chance to meet Shaw and Tiara.

Names were taken of local residents and shop owners wanting to be part of the background extras in the film, and the sewing bee ladies had added their names to the list.

Finally, Jefersen and the others arrived.

'They're here,' Hew said, phoning Daphne. 'The director and the others have arrived at the hotel. We're having the party in the next hour and I told them I'd call you so you can come and meet them. They're freshening up after their long flight.'

'Okay, Hew. We'll be there.'

The night was warm and the sun cast a mellow glow as Daphne and Ibbie walked along the main street to the hotel. Ibbie wore her new fuchsia dress and Daphne opted for a blue tea dress with a daisy print.

Ibbie chatted nervously as they approached the hotel driveway. 'I think we look presentable. I love this dress.'

'You look brilliant,' Daphne assured her.

'So do you.'

The hotel was all lit up and the sound of laughter and music wafted out the front entrance. The reception was busy with people and there was a lively party atmosphere.

Daphne took a deep breath. 'Here we go, Ibbie.'

'Don't let me say anything stupid to Shaw Starlight.'

Daphne nodded at her, and together they walked into the hotel.

The first person they saw was Jefersen, or rather, he saw them and recognised them immediately. A sexy smile lit up his handsome face.

The tall, lean but broad shouldered director approached them. He wore black jeans that emphasised his long legs and athletic thighs. The pale blue colour of his shirt complemented his sea green eyes. The sleeves were rolled up and revealed leanly muscled forearms, and his blond hair was swept back from his sculptured features. It looked like he'd recently showered and ran his hands through the thick, straight blond strands and left it to dry naturally. His light golden tan gave him a healthy glow.

Daphne's heart stuttered. Having seen his photographs online, she'd expected him to be good looking, but not this handsome. He was the most handsome man she'd ever met.

He smiled down at her and extended his hand.

'You look just like you do in your photograph, Daphne.' He seemed genuinely pleased to meet her.

Hearing him say her name in his smooth, rich, American voice made a flush rise in her cheeks.

'So do you, Jefersen,' she said. Only ten times better. 'We've been so looking forward to meeting you and Travis — and of course Shaw Starlight and Tiara Timberlane.'

'I love your Scottish accent,' he complimented her.

'I was just thinking the same about your voice,' she admitted. Though she didn't mention how it made her feel.

He smiled and shook hands with Ibbie. 'And I'd recognise you too, Ibbie. How you doin'?'

'Great. We're so excited you're actually here.'

Jefersen looked around. 'Travis was here a moment ago. There he is.' He beckoned him over.

Travis was equally tall, both around six–three, and handsome with dark hair and vivid blue eyes that had a mischievous twinkle in them. He wore blue jeans and a white shirt, again with the sleeves rolled up. He smiled at Daphne, but it was Ibbie he focused on first, shaking hands and grinning at her. There was something in his expression that made Ibbie wonder what he was thinking.

Travis exchanged a glance with Jefersen and they both looked like they were trying to suppress a grin.

'We know your secret ladies,' said Travis.

Daphne and Ibbie looked anxious.

'John sent the email.' Travis tried not to smile.

Daphne bit her lip. 'You saw the newspaper feature?'

Jefersen nodded. 'We did.'

Ibbie spoke up. 'It's my fault. I left the laptop open and John likes to snooze on it.'

'We would've told you,' Daphne said unconvincingly.

Ibbie agreed. 'One day, probably.'

Jefersen smiled. 'It's great publicity in the press, and the national media have already contacted our marketing and publicity people, so it worked. We've got the ball rolling about filming here in Scotland.'

'So you're not mad at us?' Daphne queried.

'Nope.' Jefersen smiled at her again, causing all sorts of reactions within her.

A number of people were crowded around Shaw Starlight who was signing autographs while Hew asked them to give the actor breathing room and time to enjoy the party. But Shaw seemed happy to oblige and signed every napkin and scrap of paper handed to him.

'I'll introduce you both to Shaw,' said Jefersen. 'Tiara is resting in her room and will join the party later.'

Daphne glanced at Ibbie, willing her not to swoon or saying anything silly.

'Shaw,' he called over to him. 'Come and meet Daphne and Ibbie.'

The actor headed over to them and Ibbie felt her world tilt a little.

Shaw Starlight lived up to his reputation as a Hollywood heartthrob. He had the kind of gorgeous looks that suited being on the silver screen, and a commanding presence that shone like a beacon.

Star quality, Daphne thought. That's what this man had. She was fascinated and in slight awe of meeting him, having seen him in films. There was a moment when she had to remind herself he was really here. She glanced at Ibbie who was staring unblinking at him approach, but the colour hadn't drained from her face so that was a good sign.

Shaw wore casual trousers and a shirt in cream and dark neutrals that screamed money. His dark blond hair had gold highlights and the pale blue of his eyes was stunning. He had the stature and bearing of a male model, and according to his resume he'd worked as a model before venturing into acting.

'Hi, I'm Shaw.' He shook hands with Daphne and Ibbie. 'Jefersen has told me all about you — and John.'

Daphne felt so nervous she could only smile, and yet. . .he didn't have as strong an effect on her as Jefersen. Shaw was handsome, but there was something about Jefersen that affected her in ways she hadn't felt in a long time, perhaps never.

'Where is John?' Shaw asked. 'Did you bring him with you?'

Ibbie spoke up. 'No, he's sleeping in his basket in my knitting shop.'

'Yes, Jefersen mentioned you're both businesswomen with shops in town.'

'Daphne owns the dress and fabric shop next door to me,' Ibbie explained.

'I'll have to come down and have a look about, get a feel for the town.' Shaw glanced around at the lively party. 'I like the vibe here. This is going to be a cool shoot.'

There was a lull in the crowd as Tiara Timberlane ventured down the main staircase to join the party. She looked fabulous in a figure hugging little black dress and high heels that made her slightly taller than Daphne.

Jefersen stepped forward to greet her, and Daphne felt a stab of jealousy, another unfamiliar feeling.

Tiara's blue eyes regarded Daphne and Ibbie as Jefersen introduced them. She smiled, and Daphne wondered how she'd applied her makeup so flawlessly, or had one of the makeup artists done it for her? But there was no denying that Tiara was truly beautiful.

'You look amazing,' Ibbie blurted out.

Tiara accepted the compliment casually. 'Thank you.' Then she eyed Ibbie's dress. 'I like your dress. Love the colour.'

'Daphne made it for me.'

The blue eyes turned their attention to Daphne. 'You're a designer?'

'A dressmaker.'

Tiara admired the dress again and pointed to it. 'I'll have one in cute pink and one in black.'

Daphne was taken aback. 'You want me to make you two dresses?'

'Yes. Wardrobe will give you my exact sizes, and I'll make myself available for a fitting.'

Daphne smiled tightly. 'Okay.'

A waiter came over with a tray of champagne. Shaw and Tiara accepted a glass and then left to mingle with the party crowd.

Effie, Ivy and the other women from the sewing bee were dancing with the stuntmen.

Travis held his hand out to Ibbie. 'Would you care to dance?'

Ibbie took his hand and let him lead her on to the dance floor.

Jefersen stood gazing at Daphne. 'Shall we get something to eat from the buffet? I think there's a table over there by the window. We can relax and chat about how we're going to make this movie work.'

They helped themselves to the buffet and sat down to enjoy each other's company. A waiter served their tea and coffee.

Jefersen looked at her across the table for two. There was something intimate about them being together even though it was in the midst of the party.

Ibbie was dancing happily with Travis who matched her energetic moves with a few of his own.

'I enjoy dancing,' Jefersen explained, 'but I'd prefer to have a chat with you first and relax a little.'

First? Daphne's mind whirred with the possibility that Jefersen intended dancing with her later on. She felt a surge of elation and suddenly had a greater appetite for her lemon chicken salad. She'd barely eaten anything all day. Gallons of tea and digestive biscuits didn't count.

Although Jefersen preferred coffee to tea, they'd both chosen the same food from the buffet, right down to a scoop of tomato relish and a portion of whipped cream and mayonnaise folded into grapes and blackberries topped with herbs and black pepper.

'It's a sign that we're going to get along,' he said.

She blushed. Oh how she would love to get along with a man like him, but she was realistic as well as capable of dreaming. Men like Jefersen didn't get involved with a small town dressmaker. Their lives were worlds apart, and she wasn't the type to fall for someone who would be no more than a summer fling. A broken heart wasn't on her agenda. Not this summer. Not ever again.

He was smiling at her, a sexy smile with firm lips she wanted to kiss and be damned of the consequences. She wouldn't of course.

'Tell me what you would've chosen for dessert,' he challenged her. 'If it was the same as me, I guess I'll have to consider marrying you.'

She almost choked on her food.

He laughed. 'I'm not embarrassing you, am I?'

'No, not at all,' she lied.

He was looking at her, waiting for her response. She glanced over at the selection of puddings from chocolate mousse to sticky toffee pudding. 'Tough call between the pavlova and cranachan. Probably the cranachan.'

'I'd have chosen the pavlova. I don't know what cranachan is or if I'm pronouncing it properly.'

'You're pronouncing it fine. It's a traditional Scottish dessert — raspberries, cream, oats and honey mixed with a dash of whisky.'

'Sounds delicious.'

A member of staff overheard and offered to get them two portions of cranachan which they happily accepted.

'Tell me about your shop,' said Jefersen, tucking into his chicken salad.

'It's a dressmaking and fabric shop. I make dresses and sell them, and I also buy vintage pieces for resale. The fabric sells well, and apart from local customers, I rely on my online sales. I live above the shop. It used to be a house years ago before being converted. Ibbie's knitting shop is the same. She's next door and we're situated on the main street. Have you had a chance to look at it yet?'

'We drove down it on the way here from the airport, but I'd like to walk along and get a feel for the location. Perhaps after we've had our meal, you could give me a tour. Night shoots are what I'm aiming for, so it would be ideal to view it in the evening.'

'I'd be happy to show you.' She looked out the window. 'It's such a warm night.'

'Ibbie sold me on the idea of a dark, rainy night.'

'I'm sure Scotland can accommodate you with that, though not this evening.'

'I don't want it to rain tonight. I want to enjoy being out with you.'

She blushed.

'You're blushing, Daphne.'

'You keep flattering me.'

He grinned at her.

'Enjoy your cranachan,' the staff member said serving up two portions.

Jefersen tasted a spoonful. 'This is amazing. I'll have to get the recipe to take back with me. I like to cook.'

'Do you live in Hollywood?'

'I have a house in Beverly Hills and one in Bel Air.'

'Two houses.'

'I bought one and then inherited the other from my grandfather. I use them both but sometimes I feel like I live in my office or on set.'

'There's obviously no comparison between our two lifestyles, but I know what you mean. As I live above my shop I often feel like I work non–stop. In the evenings I pack orders, deal with online sales, and sew, then get up and do it again. But I'm lucky because I love dressmaking.'

'You should come and take a break in Los Angeles. I live alone, so you'd be welcome anytime.'

She blushed. 'I know, I'm blushing.'

He laughed. 'I'm not propositioning you.'

'It sounded as if you were,' Travis said, coming over to their table.

'Where's Ibbie?' asked Daphne.

'Shaw's stunt double is dancing with her.'

Daphne looked over at the dance floor and there was Ibbie being swirled around like a toothpick by the muscled stuntman.

'I'm about to steal her back,' Travis told them. 'I just wanted to touch base and see if you two were plotting and planning great things.'

'We are. I've learned a new word, cranachan, a Scottish dessert. I keep flattering Daphne and causing her to blush. And she's promised to show me the main street after we've finished our meal.'

'Ibbie's going to show me her knitting shop, so maybe the four of us can go together.'

Jefersen smiled and nodded.

They finished their dessert, and the stunt double finally put Ibbie down. Then the foursome headed out to walk along the street.

The night was even hotter than earlier with a golden twilight casting the shops and businesses in a gilded glow.

'Hey, wait for me,' Shaw called to them. 'I want a tour of this town.'

CHAPTER SIX

Starlight and Dancing

The pubs and bar restaurant were open, but many of the shops were closed as the owners were at the hotel party.

Daphne and Ibbie gave Jefersen, Travis and Shaw a tour of the street, indicating the possibilities available.

'The street was really busy at night recently,' said Daphne, 'and lots of people were milling around. The shops were all lit up and there were more lights on than at Christmas. I looked out my bedroom window and thought — this could look like Los Angeles. I don't know what you have in mind,' she said to Jefersen, 'but I doubt you'd be here unless you thought you could make it work.'

'The UK crew sent me some rough footage they shot yesterday,' said Jefersen. 'The bar restaurant interior is something we're going to use for sure, and the camera crew filmed various shots of the street.' He pointed further along the road. 'I'm thinking that if we film from down there and angle the view so that we capture the lights on the shop fronts, it'll look great in the main three scenes involving the car chase.'

'What happens in the scenes?' Ibbie asked.

Jefersen explained. 'Tiara is kidnapped by the bad guy. We've already shot the close–ups in L.A. and we're not even going to use the featured actor. We didn't need to bring him over because the car scenes all use a stunt guy. It's Shaw and Tiara we're shooting here, and even Shaw's stunt double is working most of the scenes.'

'Dialogue is minimal on the exterior shots,' Shaw added, 'and Jefersen's style of directing creates energetic vibes. The atmosphere of his movies is terrific, and that's what he'll do here.'

Jefersen smiled at Shaw. 'The on–screen chemistry between Shaw and Tiara is electric. Audiences are going to love them. We just need to wrap them in this tight, dramatic bubble of a night filled with shadows and light and the car almost driving off with her.'

'But Shaw saves the day,' Travis concluded. 'He drives away with Tiara and the cat. An action–packed but happy ending.'

'And that's what you'll use John for?' Ibbie asked.

'Yes,' Jefersen confirmed. 'The cat will be in the car. The storyline has mentioned she's got a cat but we've not shown him, so that's why John is perfect. We initially thought a fluffy white cat would work, but having seen John's rugged appearance, he's gonna be way better.'

'When do we get to meet the cat?' said Shaw.

'You can meet him anytime,' Ibbie told him.

They'd almost reached Ibbie's knitting shop. 'That's my shop over there.'

Shaw bounded across, cupped his hand and peered through the window, impatient to see inside.

Ibbie unlocked the door. The window display lights were on and gave a glow to the little knitting shop. All of them went inside.

'He's asleep in his basket,' Ibbie whispered.

Shaw was the first to go over to have a look. 'He's snoring. I don't want to wake him. Let him sleep.'

They backed off from the cat and without invitation, Shaw ventured upstairs. Ibbie didn't mind. She was thrilled to have him in her house, and followed up after him, as did Daphne and Jefersen.

A lamp lit the living room and Shaw wandered through to the bedroom. He flicked the bedside lamp on and stood admiring Ibbie's bedroom with its mix of comfy and traditional decor.

Shaw looked around and then tried out the bed. 'Yeah, I'll sleep here tonight, soak up the atmosphere for tomorrow's shoot.' He lay on the patchwork quilt Daphne had given Ibbie as a gift. 'This is comfortable. Although I'm still firing on L.A. time, I could fall asleep here right now. Could someone have an overnight bag dropped off from the hotel?'

Travis made a call to organise it, while Ibbie wondered where she was going to sleep.

The bed was a large single, an old–fashioned style that was big enough for someone as tall as Shaw.

Ibbie and Daphne exchanged a look, and Jefersen picked up on it.

'Let's leave Shaw here and go downstairs.' Jefersen ushered them away. When they were out of earshot of Shaw, he apologised for the actor's assumption that he could sleep in Ibbie's bed.

'I don't mind, really I don't,' said Ibbie. 'But I don't have anywhere else to sleep. Daphne only has a single bed but I suppose I could sleep on the sofa.'

Travis assured her she would be given accommodation at Hew's hotel, even if someone else had to move.

Ibbie ran upstairs again, grabbed some things, put them in a bag and thought how surreal it was seeing Shaw Starlight lounging on her bed. In her dreams, she'd thought of him. But seeing him there made her realise she admired him but didn't actually fancy him.

'Let me carry your bag.' Travis lifted her bag and escorted her back to the hotel after she made sure John had something to eat and drink if he woke up during the night. But often he could snore right through until the morning, and he was sound asleep when they left. Travis also wanted to check that she secured a room. Then they planned to enjoy the rest of the party.

'Could I have a look at your shop?' Jefersen asked Daphne as they stood outside the two premises.

'Yes.' She went into her dress shop and he followed her. She thought he looked so tall standing there in the midst of her shelves of fabric and dress rails. His closeness set her senses ablaze. Everything about him pressed all her buttons, and she hoped he didn't realise the effect he had on her. 'These are the fabrics I sell, and the dresses.'

He ran an elegant hand along the length of the blue fabric with white daisy print on display. Then he looked at her dress. 'This is the same fabric.'

She nodded. 'It's a popular daisy print.' He was standing next to her, causing her heart to pound, so she put some distance between them by showing him the rest of the shop. 'And through here is the sewing room where I have the sewing bee twice a week.'

'A sewing bee?'

'A group of ladies who enjoy sewing, all sorts of dressmaking, quilting and craft sewing. We get together one evening and one night a week to sew together, share patterns and ideas, help each other and drink lots of tea and eat cakes.'

'Sounds fun, though I'm a coffee drinker and I've never sewn anything.' He noticed the roll of bright fuchsia fabric on a shelf. 'Is this the material you'll use to make Tiara's dress?'

'It is.' Daphne lifted the roll down and let him feel the soft texture of the fabric.

'This feels lovely.'

'And this is the same material in black.' There were several other colours stacked on the shelf.

'I hope you're not feeling obliged to make the dresses for Tiara. I can have wardrobe deal with what she wants if there's any pressure.'

'No, I'm happy to run the dresses up for her. I'm pleased she likes the design. I think she'll suit them.'

'These are not being made for free,' he emphasised. 'They'll be bought and paid for and for your time making them.'

'I understand, but making dresses is my job, so if Tiara Timberlane wants them, that's fine with me. I'll make a start on them tomorrow so she has a chance to wear them if she wants while she's here.'

'I'll ensure wardrobe give you the exact sizes later tonight.'

She gave him a quick look upstairs at her living room and kitchen, avoiding taking him near the bedroom, which seemed too intimate a gesture, then they went back downstairs.

Jefersen took in everything and seemed interested in seeing Daphne's world. He peered out into the garden.

Daphne opened the patio doors and the warm night air poured in.

'I like this,' he said, admiring the garden and gazing up at the sky. 'I never pictured it would feel like this in Scotland.'

'It doesn't always rain. Summers are lovely. There's often at least one heatwave during June or July. Of course, it rains as well but the seasons here are very pleasant, especially near the coast. We don't get a lot of snow, just cold, blustery days in the winter months. I suppose it's mainly sunny where you live.'

He nodded. 'I enjoy the sunshine.'

'Do you have a swimming pool?'

'Yes.'

'One in each house probably,' she said with a smile.

'Yeah. If you come over for a visit you can swim in both of them if you want.'

'It sounds like another world.'

'I guess it is, Daphne.' He sounded so thoughtful, and as he looked around, she watched him standing there in her shop, so tall and handsome. He didn't look like he belonged in her world and yet. . .she'd never met any man she'd felt so comfortable with so easily.

'Shall we head back to the party? You promised me a dance.'

'Did I?' she said.

'I'm hoping you will.'

She smiled at him and they walked together to the hotel.

The party was lively. Effie and two of the sewing bee ladies were showing the film crew how to do a Scottish reel. When they saw Daphne and Jefersen arrive, they were immediately roped into the madness. Travis was learning the steps from Ibbie.

Jefersen was a good dancer. Daphne watched him thoughtfully. He could cook, dance and make her blush.

'You've got that look again,' Jefersen told her.

She frowned. 'What look?'

'Like you're trying to figure me out.'

She didn't deny it.

They stepped aside to catch their breath and have a cool drink.

'Ask me anything you want to,' he offered. His stunning eyes showed no hint of subterfuge.

Daphne hesitated.

'Come on, anything you like.'

'Okay, why are you dancing with me? Why have you spent most of the evening with me?'

'I like you, and you're refreshingly different from the women I usually socialise with.'

'I suppose they're extremely glamorous, wealthy or work in the film industry.'

'Usually. But I have a bad reputation,' he confessed.

Daphne's heart lurched. 'You're a scoundrel?'

He laughed. 'You make me sound like a pirate or some historical cad.'

She shrugged, knowing her choice of word sounded old–fashioned. 'Are you the modern version?'

'No, I'm not.'

'What about your bad reputation?'

'You might approve of it.'

'Is it a secret?'

'No. I'm known for being difficult to date. Apparently I'm very picky and don't get involved unless I really care about someone. In my industry, I'm quite traditional when it comes to dating. I only date women I like, and haven't been involved with that many. I'm known for being a workaholic, when probably I'm just a historical cad after all.'

'Nothing wrong with working hard,' she said.

For a moment they looked at each other, and she sensed a connection with this man.

'What are you thinking, Daphne?'

'You're like a familiar stranger. We've just met and yet I feel as if. . .' She shrugged again. 'I don't know.'

He sounded out her words. 'A familiar stranger. Yes, that's how I feel about you.'

'Probably the jet lag,' she said, trying to lighten the conversation. 'It'll poleaxe you later and you'll wake up in the morning wondering why you spent the night dining and dancing with a dressmaker.'

He shook his head. 'I doubt that very much.'

She blushed, but he made no comment. He simply smiled at her and they both joined in the dancing again.

In one of the reels, Daphne ended up dancing with Travis while Ibbie was twirled around the floor by Jefersen.

'Jefersen is such a good dancer,' Daphne commented to Travis.

'He went to stage school when he was a kid. He can act too, but his real talent is writing and directing.' Then he added. 'He seems to like you.'

She blushed profusely.

'I'll take that as the feeling being reciprocated,' Travis said, grinning.

'I could say the same about you and Ibbie.'

'You certainly could, and it would be true.'

'But nothing can ever come of it surely. You're only here for two weeks at the most, then you'll be out of our lives again forever. I'd hate to see Ibbie get hurt.' She gave him a knowing look.

'I'm not that type of guy, and neither is Jefersen. Despite what people may assume about men like us, we're often looking for the same thing as you — a loving relationship and building a happy life.'

'I would've thought it would've been easy in your position. Women surely clamber after you.'

'But how many of them are real? Would you like to pin your hopes and dreams on someone who saw you as a good looking meal ticket? Or as someone who could help them get on in their career? I don't mind helping, it's a tough business, but I never want to be anyone's stepladder when it comes to settling down. And yes, that's what I want, and from knowing Jefersen for many years, that's what he eventually wants too.'

They'd stopped dancing by now and were standing amid the mayhem deep in conversation as the merriment swirled around them.

Jefersen came waltzing over with Ibbie. 'You two look so serious.'

'We're talking about love and romance,' Travis told him.

Daphne winced. These men were so open about their feelings. She wasn't quite used to their approach. She liked it, but it took a bit of getting used to. Even Hew who was quite straightforward in his liking for her, never went further than hinting that he'd like to get involved with her and settle down.

'Ah, that explains it,' said Jefersen.

Ibbie's bright eyes focussed on Travis. 'What about love and romance?'

Before he could reply, Barra approached them. In his early fifties he worked as Hew's assistant, handyman and all–round sorter of chaos, and there had been plenty during the evening.

'I've settled your man Starlight in the knitting shop,' Barra explained to them. 'He's got an overnight bag and someone from the hotel will wake him in the morning and bring him back here after his sleepover.'

'Thank you,' said Jefersen.

Ibbie still needed assurance. 'Is he actually in my bed?'

'Yes, he is, Ibbie,' Barra confirmed. 'But don't worry, he's not alone. Your wee fluff ball is snuggled up on the quilt beside him.'

'John's in Shaw's bed?' Ibbie squealed.

'He was snoring in his basket, but Mr Starlight asked me to bring him upstairs. He likes animals and wanted to bond with the cat because they're going to be filming together. Anyway, I carried him up in his basket, put him down on the bedside rug and he woke up. When he saw the strange man in your bed his fur stood on end and he was ready to fight, but then Shaw lifted him up and made friends with him. You know what John's like, he's a good–natured wee cat.'

Daphne and Jefersen laughed.

'That's fine then,' said Ibbie. 'John will wake him early in the morning. He wakes me up if I sleep through my alarm. I'll be down and ready to give him his breakfast.'

Travis grinned. 'Shaw or John?'

Ibbie laughed. 'Probably both.'

'I apologise again for Shaw imposing on you, Ibbie,' said Jefersen. 'He's used to getting what he wants.'

Ibbie stopped him apologising further. 'I understand, and it's fine by me. In fact, I would've been happy with an email reply from Hollywood, never mind having my heartthrob sleeping in my bed and cosying up to my cat.'

Travis gazed at her. 'Shaw's your heartthrob, huh?'

'He was, until I met him,' Ibbie blurted out. 'But he's different in real life. I like him but I don't fancy him, if you know what I mean.'

Travis was happy with this.

Effie, Ivy and couple of other sewing bee women came dancing over along with June and Florie.

'Where's Shaw Starlight?' asked Effie. 'He disappeared with you lot earlier and we haven't seen him since.'

'He's having a sleepover in my shop,' Ibbie explained, giving them the details.

'I'd offer to put you up for the night at my cottage,' said Effie, 'but I'm fully booked with the stuntmen.'

'So am I,' Ivy added.

'I'm staying at the hotel tonight, so don't worry,' said Ibbie. 'And John is keeping Shaw company.'

The women laughed and then continued enjoying the party, dancing with the stuntmen and some of the local men. Several of the film crew decided to get some sleep just after midnight as they had an early start the following morning, getting parts of the street ready for the evening's filming. But Jefersen and Travis continued kicking up their heels and getting to meet everyone at the party, including Ibbie's aunt and the council management.

Hew was kept busy, but every now and then Daphne saw him glance over at her. He had a resigned expression, as if realising that Daphne was interested in the director and any chance he'd had of dating her was gone.

However, Daphne was sure she noticed a spark of attraction between Florie and Hew. Even if it was mainly on Florie's part.

Tiara retired to her room having thanked Hew for his hospitality, and when Daphne and Ibbie discussed her with the other sewing bee ladies, they all agreed that although she seemed standoffish, she was okay. Hew had certainly beamed with pride as Tiara smiled at him.

'This is a copy of Tiara's dress measurements.' Travis handed Daphne a sheet of paper listing her sizes. 'Do you want payment before or after the dresses are sewn? Tiara is happy to pay in advance.'

'No, I'll make the dresses first and take the payment if she's pleased with the finished items.'

Daphne finally decided to leave the party at around 1:30 a.m. She planned to walk down the street on her own to the shop.

'I'll walk you back,' Jefersen insisted.

'I'm fine. The street is quite safe. Others are heading home as well.'

Jefersen wouldn't let her go alone, and they headed down the street together.

CHAPTER SEVEN

Sewing Bee

The night was hot with barely a breeze. Daphne looped her cardigan over her bag and was glad she'd worn the cool cotton tea dress.

They were quiet for a few moments, walking in step together, at ease in each other's company and yet. . .she was aware of how tall Jefersen was beside her, and the effect his manliness had on her.

Lost in thought for a minute, she suddenly realised he was smiling at her and laughing lightly.

'What are you smiling at?' she asked, breaking into a smile to match his.

He laughed nervously and ran a hand through the front of his hair, pushing it back. A few strands refused to be tamed, giving him a sexy appearance.

He still hadn't told her what amused him, but then he relented. 'This is like a first date. I feel so nervous.'

For a flicker of a second she saw his vulnerability behind his manly appearance.

Daphne smiled. He was right. That's exactly what it felt like.

Sea green eyes glanced down at her, gauging her reaction. Seeing her smile in agreement, he added, 'I haven't walked a girl home since high school.'

'You really don't date much, do you?' she joked.

'You got me there.'

'I've read that people mainly drive everywhere in Los Angeles, so I'm thinking you've driven quite a few women home after a date.'

'Probably a lot less than you'd imagine, but okay, I have. But with you tonight, it's like being unsure, less confidant, and I haven't felt like that in a long time.'

Someone waved to them from the window of the bar restaurant. They waved back and continued on.

'What's happening tomorrow?' Daphne asked Jefersen. 'Are you jumping right into the filming?'

'Pretty much. The film crew have sussed out several possible locations, so we'll work on those in the morning. Throughout the day we'll start initial filming with interior scenes in the bar restaurant, and then shoot a couple of exterior action scenes with the car at night. We'll need plenty of volunteers as background. I know there's a list. Wardrobe will advise on what clothes to wear. Are you taking part?'

'I'm not sure.'

'You should, but only do it if you feel comfortable being seen on screen.'

'It's a crazy situation.'

'I always think it's better to take a chance on things than risk looking back with regret.' He shrugged. 'Common sense should've prevailed when I saw Ibbie's email.' He smiled and shook his head. 'Scotland? Now that's one heck of a crazy idea.'

'I thought she pitched it well.'

'She did, and those photographs of the two of you. . .' He sighed. 'I thought, these ladies are different. They're bold and unafraid to be fun, exciting and innovative. And I decided, hell yes. We're going to Scotland.'

'I'm glad you did.'

They stopped outside her shop and he gazed down at her. 'So think about being that woman in the photograph smiling in the sunshine beside the sea. Think about taking a chance on things that seem implausible and find a way to make them work.'

'I'll try.'

He hesitated and for a moment she thought he was going to kiss her goodnight but held back.

'Goodnight, Daphne.'

'Goodnight. Thanks for a great evening.'

'No, thank you. Drop by when we're shooting tomorrow and say hi.'

She nodded but didn't promise anything. She needed time to think, to gather her thoughts and to talk to Ibbie. They hadn't had a chance to chat all night.

'Will you be okay on your own?'

She smiled pleasantly. 'I'm always on my own.' Ibbie was usually next door, but she lived and worked alone.

'What about family?' he asked.

'I've no one. I've been on my own since I was sixteen. And I've known Ibbie since school.'

'What about Ibbie?'

'She only has her mother, who never really had time for her, and still doesn't. She lives on the East Coast and hasn't even seen Ibbie's shop. It's been open for three years. They just don't get along. Never have.'

He ran a hand through his hair, wishing he hadn't brought up such difficult memories.

'Do you have family?' she said.

'Yes, loads of them. No siblings, but lots of cousins, more cousins and their kids, aunts, uncles, mom, dad, grandparents and several others whose family tree is so entwined with ours that I can't figure it out, but they've been part of our lives for years. When we get together for family celebrations, we need catering brought in.'

'I always wanted to be part of a large family. When I hear people complain about having to deal with all their relatives at Christmas, I think — I'll volunteer to go. You can stay in my shop. I'll have fun with them.'

'You should come over and join us for Thanksgiving. Then, after total chaos, perhaps rethink things.'

'Nope, I wouldn't change my mind.'

'Come over anyway. You'd be made welcome, and Ibbie.'

'I may just do that, so be careful what you offer,' she teased him.

He motioned towards the shop. 'I'll wait until you're in safely.'

She smiled to herself as she unlocked the door, went inside, locked it again and waved to him through the front window.

He waved and walked off, leaving her with an impression of him that made her like him even more.

Daphne lay in bed thinking about everything that had happened recently, thinking about Jefersen and Shaw Starlight sleeping next door in Ibbie's shop.

Ibbie sent her a text message. She read it before she fell asleep. *Travis kissed me goodnight. Just a peck but. . .details in the morning.*

Daphne rarely slept in, so she was startled to find out she'd slept through her alarm and woke up when Ibbie phoned her. She ran downstairs and let Ibbie in.

'Shaw has gone back to the hotel,' Ibbie gushed. 'He said he had a great night in my shop and gets on well with John.'

'That's wonderful. I'll have to jump in the shower and get ready to open up. And I want to hear all the details about you kissing Travis.'

'Did Jefersen make a play for you?'

'No, but he's invited me, us, to stay at his houses in Los Angeles.'

'I hope you said yes.'

'I didn't say no.'

'I'll make tea in my shop. You get dressed, then we'll chat.'

Ibbie was drinking tea when Daphne hurried in to the knitting shop.

'So, what happened with Travis?'

'He escorted me to my room at the hotel, which was lovely. I felt quite pampered. Anyway, he stepped in to make sure I had everything I needed, and as he said goodnight he leaned down and kissed me. He's a nice kisser. I'd have grabbed him and body slammed him on to the bed except I didn't want to appear forward or easy.'

Daphne sipped her tea and helped herself to a piece of shortbread.

'What happened when Jefersen walked you home?'

Daphne gave her the full version.

'Sounds as if Jefersen likes you. He certainly monopolised you at the party. Everyone from the sewing bee commented about it.'

'He's gorgeous but there's no future for me with him. He's never going to settle in Scotland, and I'm not going to live in Hollywood.'

'Why not?'

'Because my shop is here. This is where I belong.'

'What if that's not true? Neither of us have found the man we'd like to settle down with. We've nothing to show for any relationship other than a trail of disaster, and no prospects in the offing. What if Jefersen and Travis are the men for us? Or what if dating them leads to a whole new life in Los Angeles?'

'You'd really leave Scotland? Leave your knitting shop?'

'My shop is less important to me than your shop is to you. I love knitting and I like working with the yarn, but I sell it so I can make a living from something I know about. You on the other hand, are a dressmaker. You sell fabric, but you mainly sew and design dresses. I don't knit jumpers and sell them, so it would be easier for me to leave this behind. I could knit in L.A. The thing would be, how would I make a living? But if, and it's a tentative if, I was involved with Travis, maybe I could help him, work with him or—

'Marry him?'

'I'd still like my independence, and I think you would too, but we could adapt. Maybe we'd work together. You sew dresses and I sell fabric — and knit, though I doubt they'll need cosy, knitted scarves and woollies in L.A. But dresses, yes, they'd buy lovely tea dresses in wonderful fabrics. It's feasible.'

'It's not.'

'You said that about me sending the email, and look what's happened since then.'

'Okay,' Daphne relented. 'But what are the chances of both of us finding love with men like Jefersen and Travis?'

'Did you see the way Jefersen looks at you? The man's smitten. And unless I'm mistaken, Travis likes me. We're different to the women in L.A. We're just us, down to earth and yet adventurous. I know we're not as beautiful as Tiara Timberlane, but few women are. Not to toot our own horn too loud, but we're okay.'

'Jefersen and Travis are really handsome, and wealthy. They could have lots of women who fit their lifestyles.'

'They could, but obviously they haven't had any luck or they wouldn't be single and making a play for us, would they?'

There was a weird logic in what Ibbie said.

'I love my shop,' said Daphne.

'So do I, but I'd also like to find a nice man, someone who isn't a Duncan. Travis is lovely.'

'Let's take things easy. Maybe it was a first flush of excitement. We'll see what happens as they start filming.'

'But we'll stay open to flirting, kissing and any offers that we trust.'

'Agreed.'

Effie came hurrying in. 'The wardrobe people have asked if the sewing bee can help sew some of the clothes for the extras to wear in the background. I've rounded up the girls and wondered if it would be okay to use your sewing room.'

'Yes, they're welcome. I'll set up the sewing machines,' said Daphne, running off to get things ready. Effie hurried after her.

'It's not full garment work, just alterations to items that are blatantly not suitable — unpicking logos from jackets and tops, stitching on other logos and the odd badge. They hadn't expected so many people to volunteer to take part and are a bit overwhelmed.'

'I'm sure we can help them,' said Daphne, flicking on every sewing machine she had, including the one she used in the front shop.

'They gave me a list of the items needing altered.' Effie pinned the list up in the sewing room.

Daphne skimmed the list. 'Yes, we can handle this.'

'People taking part in the film were asked to bring the clothes they intended wearing, mainly jeans or casual trousers, tops and jackets, so that wardrobe could confirm if they fitted in with the film's styling. Most of them passed fine, but just by sheer numbers of volunteers, the wardrobe people ended up with a load of items needing altered. It was Travis who suggested the sewing bee help them. Ibbie had been explaining all about us last night.'

'Ibbie got on well with Travis,' Daphne commented, setting out a selection of thread and scissors.

Effie grinned. 'So did you and Jefersen. You two looked very cosy.'

Daphne blushed.

'He's a handsome one.'

'Who is?' Ivy said, bustling in ready to help.

'Jefersen,' said Effie. 'We were just talking about how Daphne and Ibbie have captured the attention of the director and Travis.'

'Oh yes,' Ivy agreed. 'Those men are smitten. And why shouldn't they be? Our girls are gorgeous, talented and have lovely natures. They're also sheer troublemakers. I mean, look what we're all involved in with their meddling, but faint heart never won a handsome man worth having.'

Effie smiled. 'I think they're quite taken with you and Ibbie's boldness. You're both down to earth but willing to aim for the stars.'

'Speaking of stars,' said Ivy, 'how did Shaw Starlight enjoy his night in Ibbie's shop?'

'He loved it,' Daphne confirmed. 'And he's made friends with John.'

Several ladies arrived, armed with their sewing gear. By mid–morning the bee was buzzing with activity.

Barra rushed in brandishing a note for Daphne. 'One of the crew's organisers asked me to give you this.'

'What is it?'

'It's a note telling you to list all the fabrics, thread and other items you use for the clothes alternations.' Barra looked around. 'They said you were helping them out, and payment is being made for sundries so no one, especially you and your shop, is out of pocket. They've ordered cakes from Nairna's bakery to be sent to keep you all going.'

'Lovely,' said Daphne. 'We would've helped them anyway.'

Barra shrugged. 'They insisted you get paid. The film has a wardrobe budget and that's how they like to do things.'

'Fair enough.' Daphne put the note on her shop counter, intending to list anything used, though from what they'd been doing so far, it was more actual sewing than using fabrics, and she didn't mind providing the thread.

'Hew says I've to help you as well,' Barra told Daphne. 'Is there anything else you need before I go back up to the hotel?' He glanced around. 'How about milk for the tea. You'll be drinking lots to keep you going. I could pop to the grocery shop for a couple of big cartons.'

Daphne accepted his offer. 'Yes, milk would be handy. Thanks, Barra.'

He ran off to get it while the sewing continued.

Daphne opened the patio doors. The day was getting warmer.

Numerous clothing items were piled on one of the tables and the ladies systematically picked one up, read the alternation needed which was pinned to each garment, and set about sorting it.

Florie ran between her quilt shop and the sewing bee, helping them out. Ibbie made a round of tea for everyone which they enjoyed with the fresh cream sponge cakes and cupcakes from Nairna's bakery.

Effie told the ladies about the stuntmen while she stitched. 'I don't need to attend to them today. They're rehearsing the car stunts and getting fed at the hotel.'

'Shaw Starlight's stunt double is a sexy beast,' one of the ladies said while snipping the threads of her sewing. 'I've seen Shaw's films before and I looked them up online last night. The stunt double has worked on other films with him. I think he was the man who fought with a huge sword in one of the big fight scenes in the adventure epic that was a hit a couple of summers ago.'

'I remember that film,' said Ibbie. 'Shaw's blond hair was extra long for that part, almost down to his shoulders. He looked wild and sexy.'

The women agreed, and they continued to chat, sew and enjoy their tea and cakes until the afternoon when they'd cleared the backlog of items.

Daphne also cut out the pattern pieces for Tiara's two dresses and made a start on them. Local sales in her shop were next to nothing as everyone was too busy getting ready for the filming, but her online sales continued and so Daphne had to parcel up items to be posted off to her customers.

A member of the film crew stopped by to ask them to illuminate their shop windows from five o'clock onwards as they were filming one of the car stunt scenes.

'Light up your windows with anything you have. The details won't show as the car will be driving past at speed,' he said.

'Would fairy lights be okay?' Daphne asked him.

'Yes, the main thing is to create a well–lit background of shops as the car whizzes by,' he said. 'Use any lights you have.'

Daphne and Ibbie dug out their Christmas decorations and hung the fairy lights in their front windows and around the shop doors.

Ibbie stood back to admire their handiwork. 'These will light up like beacons when it's dark.'

Travis came striding down the street and waved to Ibbie and Daphne.

Ibbie's heart thundered when she saw him. 'He looks luscious,' she whispered to Daphne.

Daphne had seen Ibbie fall for various men, but Travis was easily the most handsome. She hoped Travis did like her friend and wasn't just one more broken heart in the making. And yet. . . the way he smiled warmly when he saw Ibbie gave her hope that his intentions were genuine. She liked Travis. He seemed like a nice guy.

'Can we borrow John?' Travis asked Ibbie. 'We're rehearsing one of the scenes with Tiara where she's supposed to have the cat. She hasn't even met John yet, so could I take him along to her? We're setting up the car shots for tonight.'

'He was here a minute ago,' said Ibbie.

'He's snoozing in the garden,' Effie told them. 'We gave him a saucer of milk and then he wandered out into the sunshine.'

Ibbie called out to him. 'John.'

His ears pricked up hearing her call his name. He opened his eyes and saw her waving at him.

'Come on, John, come on,' she beckoned him.

John stretched, yawned and then padded over to her. She lifted him up. 'Maybe I should go with you until we see how he reacts meeting Tiara. Is she a cat person?'

'She adores cats,' Travis assured her. 'But please bring him along.' He gave John a clap on the head. 'Hi, buddy. How you doin?'

John purred loudly, relishing the attention.

'We'll keep an eye on your shop,' said Daphne.

'They make a lovely couple,' Effie commented as they walked away together.

Daphne watched them through the shop window. They did. Ibbie and Travis looked like a couple. Of all the men Ibbie had dated, she suited walking beside Travis, both of them chatting happily and playing with John.

'You'll miss her if she leaves Scotland to make a new life with him in Hollywood,' Ivy said to Daphne.

A stab of regret shot through Daphne. She would miss Ibbie. They'd been together as best friends for years, grown up together. Somehow she always thought that when they both found men they were happy with and got married, they'd continue being in each other's lives. She'd assumed they'd live locally and would see each other all the time. The thought of being apart made her heart ache, and yet she would always put her friend's happiness first.

Ivy saw the look on Daphne's face. 'You could still keep in touch by phone and online and visit once or twice a year.'

Daphne felt suddenly teary which was ridiculous. She mentally scolded herself. If Ibbie left with Travis they would still be friends. They'd always be friends, even if they lived on opposite sides of the world.

CHAPTER EIGHT

Romance and Fun

Tiara Timberlane sat outside the bar restaurant going over the script with Jefersen.

Shaw rehearsed part of the car chase scene with his stunt double. The car was parked near the bar restaurant. Shaw was determined to do part of the stunt himself, and mats were put down to break his fall as the stand–in for the villain wrestled Shaw for control of the car. They had to roll across the bonnet of the black sports car, throw a few punches at each other, and when Shaw gained the upper hand, the villain would run off leaving Shaw free to rescue Tiara. She was to be tied up in the back seat of the car with the cat.

Travis explained this part of the storyline to Ibbie as they walked up to Tiara and Jefersen.

'It sounds exciting,' said Ibbie, 'especially as this is the scene with John in it.'

'They may use John in other scenes, depending on how he comes across in the dailies — the footage that's viewed every day from the shoot,' said Travis.

Jefersen smiled when he saw Ibbie. 'Hi, come and join us. Tiara wants to meet John.'

Tiara got up, put her script down on her chair and eyed the cat.

'This is Tiara, John,' Ibbie said coaxing him to acknowledge her.

'He looks just like his pictures in the press,' said Tiara.

Ibbie wasn't sure if this was a good thing or not.

'Would you like to hold him?' Ibbie offered John to Tiara.

At first she was reluctant to take him, but as he settled easily into her arms she smiled down at him.

Ibbie glanced at Travis and they both sighed with relief.

John purred loudly, content with Tiara.

'He likes you,' said Jefersen.

Tiara nodded. 'Yeah, he does.'

They continued the rehearsals and included John who played his part well. All he had to do was look as if he was Tiara's cat, and sit beside her in the car.

The day faded to early evening and those who were taking part in the filming started to gather ready for shooting preliminary scenes. Camera crew tested the light, adjusted the equipment, adapted to their surroundings, while Jefersen directed everything and viewed the action regularly through the cameras himself.

Wardrobe staff had distributed the clothes the sewing bee had helped with, and a feeling of excitement filled the air. Lights shone from every shop in the street, and as the twilight descended upon the town, everyone got ready for the first full–on shoot.

Travis was busy assisting Jefersen, organising the stunt doubles and Shaw, while Ibbie sat on one of the crew's canvas chairs and watched the whole scenario.

Daphne joined her.

'I'm sorry,' a crew member said to them, 'but can you ladies take your places in your shops please? We're about to roll.'

As everyone was busy participating, Daphne and Ibbie didn't feel they could refuse, so they hurried along to their shops and stood in the window of Ibbie's knitting shop watching the action.

It was only when the car drove past their shops, heading further along the street, followed by a camera crew, that they realised something.

'We probably look like the mannequins in your dress shop,' said Ibbie.

Daphne laughed, realising she was right.

The car turned at the far end of the street, and then came driving back along.

'Stand close to the window,' Ibbie said hurriedly. 'Pose like a mannequin.'

Daphne went along with Ibbie's silly idea. 'They won't be able to see us. We'll be a blur along with the lights.'

'It doesn't matter. When we watch the film in the cinema, we'll remember we were there. And you never know, perhaps there will be a glimpse of us.'

Daphne doubted it. The crew member had assured them when they'd talked about putting lights in the window that no details would be picked up. The fact that she was standing in the window with Ibbie was just a daft notion, something they'd giggle at when they saw the finished film.

They continued to stand in the window display as it gave them a great view of the filming in the street.

'I wonder how John is getting on?' said Ibbie.

'What did Tiara think of him?'

'She liked him. There was a moment when I thought she wasn't pleased that he wasn't cute, but then they bonded really well. When they were rehearsing tying her up, he was very protective of her. I had to hold him so he didn't take a swipe at the stuntman. They thought it was quite funny, but you know how protective John is if he likes you.'

'Yes, but at least that means he'll be happy working with Tiara.'

'Exactly.'

'Here they come again,' said Ibbie. 'Let's wave this time.'

'No, don't, it might cause a distraction.'

'Nonsense. Come on, Daphne, give them a wave.'

So she did.

'You're going to get us in trouble,' said Daphne. 'Look, there's Jefersen with the camera crew. Do you think he saw us misbehaving?'

'No, he's too busy concentrating on the filming,' Ibbie assured her. 'He's not even looking over at us.'

Daphne went to step out of the window display, but Ibbie pulled her back. 'You'll miss all the fun.' She pointed along towards the grocery shop. 'Oh my goodness, look at Effie and the girls, they're all dressed up and faffing about the street.'

Daphne peered out. 'Is that Ivy in a lovely summery dress?'

Ibbie focussed. 'It is. For a moment I thought it was Florie. I think she's wearing one of Florie's dresses. Yes, I'm certain she is. And she looks fantastic with her hair done in a softer style. Go Ivy!'

They both waved, and Effie saw them, nudged the others and they all waved over to the knitting shop.

Ibbie sighed. 'It makes me wish now we'd agreed to be part of the background for these scenes.'

'I prefer watching from the window.'

'But we're included in tomorrow night's filming. I promised Travis.'

'Promised him what?' Daphne sounded concerned.

'They need two fit women wearing skimpy clothes to dive out of the way of the car during the second chase scene. The car will drive past our shops and all we have to do is dive over the bonnet and land on the safety mats.'

'What?' Daphne shrieked.

'I thought it would be quite exciting. I told them we're always up for a bit of fun.'

Daphne looked distraught. 'I'm not doing that.'

Ibbie burst out laughing. Daphne realised she'd been winding her up.

'I was just joking, Daph.'

As they stood in the window, Daphne playfully grabbed Ibbie's throat and pretended to strangle her. Ibbie couldn't stop laughing.

The stunt car drove past as they were doing this.

Neither of them knew they'd been captured on film until Jefersen viewed the footage.

'Take a look at this,' Jefersen said to Travis.

Travis watched the playback screen and laughed. 'They're nothing but trouble.'

'I think I might keep it in the movie.'

'Perhaps you should.'

Jefersen nodded. 'Yeah, maybe I'll do that.'

Effie, Ivy and several other sewing bee ladies stood outside the bar restaurant watching Tiara Timberlane relax in her chair while the car stunt was set up again. John sat on her lap having his ears rubbed.

'Tiara's quite taken with John,' Ivy commented. 'Mind you, he's got a good nature.'

Effie agreed. 'John's quite happy with her. He'd sense if she was a bad apple.'

'Speaking of which. . .' Ivy motioned to a couple in the crowd across the street. 'Duncan and his girlfriend having been watching everything. But they're not taking part in any of the filming. The grocer told me it's because Ibbie initiated it.'

'Ach, stuff them. Duncan's such a sour face and so is she. He lost a lovely, bright, young woman when he ditched Ibbie.'

Ivy looked along the road. 'Where are Daphne and Ibbie?'

Effie had no idea. 'Up to mischief no doubt.'

The ladies admired Shaw Starlight, standing beside his stunt double, talking animatedly to Jefersen.

'They're all fine looking men, aren't they?' said June.

'They certainly are,' Effie agreed. 'Shaw has star quality but there's something rugged about his double that I prefer.'

Ivy admired him. 'He's lovely, isn't he? I was watching him and the other stuntmen training hard on the shore from my kitchen window. I was boiling up a big pot of tatties for them. They were running along the sand then practising their martial arts and fighting. Not real fighting obviously. They're very skilled. It was impressive to watch.'

'It's interesting to see how they work,' said Effie. Then she noticed Jefersen conferring with the stunt crew. 'The stunt coordinator looks as if he's reorganising things with Jefersen and Shaw.' She motioned across to where they setting up the car. 'I wonder if they're going to try something different?'

As they watched, Shaw insisted on doing another stunt.

'It would add to the drama,' Shaw said to Jefersen. 'We've rehearsed moves like this before. You know I can do this.'

The stunt coordinator spoke confidently. 'Shaw can handle this.' He went on to discuss bringing in the villain's double. 'By filming him from behind, focussing on Shaw lifting up Tiara when's she's tied up and being kidnapped, we could expand on the action.'

'Okay, let's do it,' said Jefersen.

Everything was set up. The main action took place when the car spun around to a halt. Shaw and the villain were supposedly fighting for control of the car. Tiara was in the back seat with John.

When the car stopped, Shaw and the villain tumbled from the vehicle, fighting. Shaw gained the upper hand and punched his attacker unconscious. While he regained his senses, Shaw lifted Tiara out of the car, rescuing her from the clutches of the bad guy in an action–packed scenario.

Several cameras captured it from all angles, and it seemed to go well on the first take, which is what they'd hoped for. Unfortunately, no one had taken into account the cat's reaction. Thinking Tiara was being taken against her will, John pounced into action. Paws flailing, he dived at Shaw, grabbing on to his back and climbing up to his shoulders, trying to bite, scratch and force him to let go of Tiara.

Fortunately, Shaw's leather jacket protected him from most of the onslaught, but when John climbed on to the actor's head from the rear he felt the wrath of the protective kitty.

Jefersen kept his arm up indicating to the camera crew to keep rolling for a couple of seconds before they cut.

The moment Shaw put Tiara down, John jumped off his head to check if she was okay and then looked furiously up at Shaw, warning him off.

Shaw was good–natured about the whole thing. 'Okay, buddy, I'm backing off.' He stepped away.

Jefersen hurried over to one of the cameras desperate to view the playback.

The crew held their breath, hoping they'd captured some useable footage, though no one was expecting the cat attack to be workable. They geared up to reshoot the final part of the action.

'This is great!' Jefersen announced, beckoning Shaw and Travis to view the footage.

'Wow! Look at that little guy give me hell,' announced Shaw. 'Can we use this?' he asked Jefersen.

'Oh, yeah.' Jefersen grinned at John who was now snuggling into Tiara. The director glanced around. 'Anyone know where Daphne and Ibbie are? They need to see this. It's wonderful.'

'They'll be in their shops. I'll go get them.' Travis hurried away.

Ibbie saw him approach. She waved to him through the knitting shop window. 'Here's Travis.'

Daphne peered out. He was smiling so she assumed he hadn't seen them in the background of the film scene.

Ibbie opened the door.

'Come and see John in action,' he said to them.

They hurried with him to where Jefersen was viewing the footage. He grinned when he saw them.

Daphne's heart fluttered seeing him.

'Have a look at John.' Jefersen pulled Daphne close, putting his arm around her in a casual gesture to show her the playback, but it sent her senses wild. 'You too, Ibbie.' He made room for both of them.

Daphne watched the footage while aware of how exciting and comforting it felt being pressed against Jefersen's chest with his arm around her shoulder. He was leaning in, pointing to the screen.

'This is where Shaw rescues Tiara,' he explained. 'When he picks her up, John thinks he's hurting her and starts to defend her.'

'Oh my goodness,' said Ibbie. 'Did anyone get hurt? Is John okay? Is Shaw all right about being attacked?'

'Yeah, everything's fine,' Jefersen assured. 'No one got harmed, especially John. He settled down almost immediately. And Shaw's jacket protected him from being clawed. By the time John had clambered up on to the back of his head, we cut the filming. It's perfect. We're going to use it. Audiences will wonder how the heck we got a cat to act on cue. You can feel the affection he has for Tiara and his all–out action to defend her.' Jefersen paused, picturing his vision of the movie. 'I can see this being in the trailer. People will love it.'

'What do you think?' Travis asked Ibbie. She stepped away from the camera to chat to him while Daphne remained with Jefersen.

Jefersen kept his arm around Daphne's shoulder and smiled. 'I'm so glad John emailed me.'

'It's going to give your film a whole new dimension,' said Daphne.

He smiled warmly, gazing at her as he spoke softly. 'And I got to meet you.'

She felt the heat rise deep within her, and was sure he sensed how he unsettled her. She didn't step away, didn't move. She wanted to keep this moment of intimacy between them. Even when surrounded by people milling about in the street, she was in her own little bubble with Jefersen.

He leaned closer and at first she thought he was going to kiss her, but instead he whispered in her ear, sending further sensations through her as he swept her hair aside. She felt his breath brush against the side of her face as he said, 'And you're going to be in the movie too. You and Ibbie.'

She pulled back and gazed up at him, still close, near enough to see the amused twinkle in his beautiful eyes.

'You saw us in the shop window?' she said hesitantly.

'Oh, yeah. And I'm keeping it in for posterity and because I want to. It kinda sums up you and Ibbie.'

She bit her lip. 'In a good way?'

He nodded and took hold of her hand, clasping it in his. No one else could see this. The simple touch of his hand, claiming hers, wanting to be close, made her heart ache to be even closer to him.

'I've never met anyone like you, Daphne. I know I never will again.'

And then he leaned down and kissed her.

His lips felt warm, firm, sensual. Lost to everything except the moment, Daphne kissed him back. He wrapped his arms around her and pulled her to him, before releasing her.

Perhaps it was only a second, the briefest moment, but Daphne neither knew nor cared whether anyone had seen Jefersen kiss her. She heard the sound of chatter and laughter and people busying themselves around them, and yet between her and Jefersen, all she could really hear was the excited beat of her heart.

'This will never work,' she murmured.

'I'm going to figure out a way to make it work,' he promised her.

She'd had promises from men before, men she thought she cared about but they'd all deceived her in some way or let her down. Jefersen's promise she hoped would be different. She believed he was genuine. She'd felt the attraction to him as soon as they'd met, and when she'd seen his picture online her heart had reacted at first glance. And why not? Jefersen was so handsome.

'The bar restaurant is ready,' one of the camera crew called to Jefersen.

He gave the guy the thumbs up, while still holding Daphne's hand.

'Want to be in the restaurant scene? You're looking real pretty in that dress.'

She hesitated, but Ibbie came bounding over with Travis in tow.

'Travis has persuaded me to be part of the restaurant background,' Ibbie chirped. 'Come on, Daphne.'

Jefersen let go of Daphne's hand as Ibbie clasped it and pulled her friend into the bar restaurant.

Daphne went along with her, still full–hearted from kissing Jefersen.

Ibbie led the way through the bar to the restaurant area where they sat down at a table ready to have their meal served.

Ibbie grinned at her and kept her voice low. 'I saw you kissing Jefersen.'

Daphne's face flushed bright pink. 'Did anyone else notice?'

'No one except everyone who was standing near the pair of you. The two of you were lost to the world. Smooching like you were under the moon.'

Daphne cringed. 'It's so embarrassing.'

'No it's not, silly. I'd have seen whether you kissed him first or if it was the other way around if I hadn't let Travis plant a kiss on me.'

Daphne laughed. 'You were kissing Travis again?'

Ibbie reacted excitedly. 'He's so smoochable. Kissing Travis is going to be my new summer hobby.'

A frown crossed Daphne's smooth brow. 'Are you okay about being involved with him if it's just a summer romance?'

'Well I'm certainly not going to give a gorgeous man like Travis the flick just because there's a chance it won't go the distance. But it might. You never know. Put it this way, how many useless prats have we pinned our hopes on during past summers only to have them cast us aside?'

'A few.' It was slightly higher, but she didn't want to highlight this.

'So what's the difference? Let's enjoy dating two handsome American hunks while the sun shines and we're taking part in a Hollywood film. This is the stuff that dreams are made of. You don't get a second chance at living out a fantasy. I'm telling you right now, I'm going for it, Daphne. I really am. And you should too. You deserve some happiness with a real man instead of those selfish eejits you're inclined to get involved with.'

Two steak dinners were put down in front of them, piping hot.

'Thanks,' Ibbie said to the waiter.

'This is a proper meal,' Daphne commented.

'The bar restaurant owner is being fully compensated by the film company,' said Ibbie. 'The kitchen staff are busy cooking up loads of dinners for everyone so the restaurant looks busy. If they served up fake food it wouldn't have the same atmosphere.'

Daphne looked around. People at several tables were tucking into their meals. Effie, Ivy and the sewing bee ladies, along with Florie and Nairna were among those taking part.

'We're not to wave over at each other,' said Ibbie. 'Travis says we have to look natural, like we're out for an evening meal in L.A.'

Daphne noticed they'd changed some of the decor, replacing local items with American style signs and accessories. 'They've really created a great look for this.'

'They have. The set crew have a ton of stuff in one of their big trailers and tarted this place up to look like an American joint.' Ibbie sighed. 'Wouldn't it be fantastic to go to Hollywood? Maybe we'll take Jefersen up on his invitation to visit him. Two houses, eh?'

Ibbie started to eat her French fries and Daphne decided to join her. All of a sudden she felt hungry. The steak dinner with all the trimmings smelled and tasted delicious. The local chefs had made a great job of rustling up the authentic looking meals.

'Everyone ready?' Travis called to them. 'We're filming the first take.'

'And action!' Jefersen announced.

The camera captured the scene, a busy bar restaurant, as Shaw and Tiara made their entrance. Shaw led Tiara over to a vacant table, then headed to the bar. While he was ordering their drinks, the villain's double made a forceful play for Tiara, who shrugged off his advances. Shaw then confronted him and the two men took their fight outside.

'Cut!' shouted Jefersen.

They shot the scene again, capturing different angles and making sure the confrontation between Shaw and his adversary was even stronger.

Everyone played their part. No silly waving. No spoiling the scene. Jefersen thanked them all for their participation.

Daphne had been so wrapped up in the whole scenario she hadn't realised she'd scoffed most of her dinner. Ibbie had done the same.

'That was incredible to watch,' said Daphne. 'Seeing Shaw act like that was amazing.'

'He's such a smashing actor, as well as being sexy gorgeous.'

'Speaking of sexy gorgeous, here's your hot summer date,' Daphne whispered to Ibbie as Travis approached them.

Ibbie giggled.

'What are you two laughing about?' asked Travis.

'Nothing,' Ibbie said smirking. 'We were just enjoying the fun of the filming.'

Travis threw her a knowing smile. He didn't believe a word she said.

Ibbie sighed. 'Okay, we were talking about sexy gorgeous men.'

'I guess I've got tough competition.'

Daphne spoke up. 'No Travis. None at all as far as Ibbie's concerned.'

It was Ibbie's turn to blush.

Travis grinned then Jefersen waved him over.

Daphne finished her food and smirked.

'I can't believe you said that to him,' Ibbie chided her, although secretly pleased.

Daphne shrugged. 'It's true.'

'I know it's true, but—'

'But nothing. It's obvious Travis likes you.'

'He seems to.'

Daphne nodded and smiled at her.

And then they giggled and chatted about love, romance and sewing as the filming continued.

'Can I buy you two ladies a drink?'

They looked up and saw the stunt coordinator standing at their table smiling at them.

Taken aback, they hesitated.

'Effie has told me all about you,' he said. 'We haven't had a chance to meet. It's been a hectic shoot, but I wanted to meet the two women responsible for this.'

'I'll have a glass of wine,' said Ibbie. 'And we've heard a lot about you. Effie says you're. . .' She stopped, trying to filter out the blatant compliments especially about the stuntmen's sexy builds.

He looked down, waiting on what she had to say.

'She says you keep fit running along the shore,' said Ibbie.

'It's a beautiful part of the country,' he said. 'I enjoy the coast, all the fresh air and swimming in the sea. I suppose you enjoy it too, from the photographs of you in your swimsuits.'

'Yes,' said Daphne. 'We try to make the most of the summer when the sun's out.'

'I hope you'll come down and join us. We're training tomorrow morning bright and early. If you're up, come down for a swim and some exercise.'

Daphne and Ibbie smiled, nodded in a non–committal way, and waited until he'd gone before gasping in awe at being invited to train with the stuntmen.

CHAPTER NINE

Cakes and Sewing

Travis came over to Daphne and Ibbie's table.

'Jefersen is pleased with the scenes but there are parts he wants to reshoot to work in with the new aspects he's adding to the storyline,' Travis explained.

'Do you want us to sit here in the restaurant?' asked Ibbie.

'Yes, and Jefersen's bringing in a camera from over there near the bar and sweeping across the restaurant, so if you could ignore what's going on and continue to look natural that would be helpful.'

'We'll do that,' Daphne assured him.

Travis smiled and lingered for a moment, as if he wanted to say something but it was awkward.

'Everything okay?' Ibbie asked him.

'Yes, it's just. . .I don't want to come across as the jealous boyfriend type because I'm not. . .'

The main word Ibbie heard was *boyfriend.* Her wide green eyes gazed up at him.

'I sort of overheard you getting invited to spend time tomorrow morning with the stunt guys.' Travis shrugged, but his manner was still awkward. 'They're great guys, but. . .'

'I get it,' said Ibbie.

'I mean, sure, go have fun with them,' he said, trying to sound nonchalant.

A camera crew member waved him over, asking for his assistance.

Travis smiled at Ibbie and Daphne. 'Catch you later.'

Daphne grinned at Ibbie. '*Boyfriend.*'

Ibbie was all a flutter. 'Are my cheeks burning?'

'They are.'

Ibbie fanned herself with a dinner napkin. 'You're usually the blushing one between us, but just the way he looked at me. . . Although I don't like really possessive and jealous men, it's flattering if they're a wee bit miffed if another man intervenes.'

Daphne agreed. 'My ex is a prime example of not having a jealous bone in his body. I thought at first it was a good thing, then I realised it was more that he didn't give a toss about me.'

Ibbie leaned forward in her chair and confided to Daphne. 'Do you know what I was thinking about last night when I was in my bed, trying to get some sleep, but still buzzing after Travis kissed me goodnight?'

Daphne's blue eyes were wide with interest. 'No, what?'

'Every boyfriend I've ever had, I've known for ages before actually dating them.'

Daphne thought about this. 'Yes, you and Duncan flirted but it was a while before he asked you out.'

'Almost a year. I think the same thing applies to you. You definitely knew two of your ex–boyfriends for several months before you started going out with them.

'That's true,' Daphne agreed.

'So I wondered if the rules for romance work in the opposite direction for us. You're supposed to get to know a man, decide if he's okay, and then start dating him. But when we do that, every relationship has been a disaster. It doesn't work for us. Maybe becoming involved with Travis and Jefersen now is exactly what we need.'

'Perhaps you're right, but it's still crazy to think about romance with men from Hollywood. Jefersen says he's going to find a way to make it work, but. . .' Daphne shrugged.

'Their work and backgrounds are an open book online. We've checked them out. There doesn't seem to be any outrageous scandal. They've dated but don't seem to have found women they want to settle down with, and from the things Travis has said, he's at a point in his life when he's looking to settle.'

'Is that what you want though, Ibbie?'

Daphne sometimes wondered if her friend preferred being carefree.

'I know I come across as a wildcard, a firecracker, but yes, I do want to settle down. There are nice men around here, but we've never dated them. They always find someone else and we're left on the shelves like remnants of fabric that are quite pretty but no one actually wants, not here anyway. I don't want to be the bright patterned fabric that becomes faded with time. I'm sure you don't either.'

'You know I don't. But our shops — we love our shops.'

'Our shops are our anchors. They keep us financially safe, but they also pin us down.'

Daphne loved her shop, but after three years of non–stop work, she often longed for the ability to relax a bit. They closed for the holidays at Christmas and New Year, but only for a few days, and even then they had to restock the shops after the Christmas chaos. Often she only got a couple of days snatched here and there, but this was part of owning her own business.

'Your dressmaking skills are first class. You could set up in business anywhere.'

Steak dinners were served up again, interrupting their conversation.

'Everyone ready for filming?' Travis announced.

'I'm not as hungry as I was,' Ibbie said to Daphne.

Neither was Daphne.

Travis walked by and stole one of Ibbie's French fries. 'Just checking they're hot enough,' he joked, then walked on, casting a cheeky grin over his shoulder at her.

'I do like Travis,' said Daphne.

Ibbie picked up a French fry. 'He's certainly hot enough.' She popped it in her mouth as the cameras started rolling.

The fight between Shaw and the bad guy was packed with more fisticuffs, and although Daphne knew they were pulling their punches, she couldn't help but wince watching them.

Ibbie giggled. 'They're only kidding on.'

'I know, but it's very realistic.'

Just then a loud meow sounded from the entrance to the bar restaurant. The doors were open wide and John had seen the skirmish. Thinking it was real, he flew at the bad guy, this time defending Shaw from being attacked. John hadn't liked Shaw manhandling Tiara, but they'd been sleepover buddies and now he was willing to stop Shaw from taking a beating.

Jefersen signalled the camera crew to keep filming, while John joined in the fray.

Shaw, the stuntman and the cat tumbled in a flurry of fists, fury and fur into the street where Jefersen finally shouted, 'Cut!'

Shaw and the stuntman got up laughing at the antics of the cat.

'Yeah, John,' Jefersen said, applauding the cat whose fur was standing on end as he prowled beside Shaw, keeping the stuntman at bay.

Shaw bent down and patted John. 'Thanks, buddy.' Then he grinned at Jefersen. 'You gotta love that cat.'

Ibbie watched to see if John was okay and relaxed when Travis nodded over to her that everything was fine.

'John's done well getting in on the action,' said Daphne.

'Whatever they're paying him, I think he's earning it,' Ibbie added.

Every now and then John looked over at Ibbie and Daphne, checking that they were okay.

Jefersen and Travis viewed the footage and then Travis announced to those taking part in the background. 'We got what we needed folks. You can relax, enjoy the food or go home if you want. Thanks again.'

No one went home.

Effie came over to Daphne and Ibbie's table.

'How are the romances going?' Effie asked, then grinned at Daphne. 'I saw you smooching with Jefersen.'

'We're doing fine,' Daphne told her.

'More than fine by the way you were welded to the director's lips.'

Ibbie laughed.

'And you can laugh, Ibbie. The girls have been watching all the flirting going on between you and Travis.'

'Did you put the stunt coordinator up to inviting us to the shore tomorrow morning?' said Ibbie.

'No, it wasn't me, it was Ivy. She told him that you two girls were single, unattached and looking for love.'

Daphne gasped. 'She what?'

'That was before she knew the two of you fancied Jefersen and Travis,' Effie explained. 'She probably didn't phrase it quite so bluntly. I think she only wanted to make sure you got a chance to meet them and have a wee bit of fun.'

'Travis overheard, and he was jealous. But he tried to backtrack and hide it,' said Daphne.

'Oh! Ibbie. I think you've got a hot romance on your agenda this summer.'

'Yes, Effie, I think you're right.'

'We'll have to find time to catch up on all the gossip,' said Effie.

'Pop round to my shop tomorrow afternoon,' Daphne suggested.

Effie sounded excited. 'I'll tell the girls. We'll bring our sewing and cakes. I'll bake us a strawberry and whipped cream sponge cake.'

'Cakes and sewing — the perfect combination,' said Daphne.

Effie hurried back to her table to tell the others.

Jefersen approached Daphne and Ibbie.

'We're rehearsing a few more shots and taking John with us, but would you care to join Travis and me for a drink later at the hotel?'

'Yes,' said Daphne.

'Great. We'll see you there around eleven–thirty.'

Daphne smiled and nodded.

Jefersen walked away.

'A double date, Daphne. We've never had one of those before.'

'This will be really great or a total farce.'

'Does it matter as long as we enjoy ourselves?'

Daphne leaned back in her chair. 'I guess not.'

Daphne and Ibbie walked up to the hotel later.

'I'm feeling nervous,' Daphne admitted.

'So am I. Do I look nervous?'

'No, you look perky.'

'I should look blooming exhausted, and so should you. We've been on the go since early this morning, but I feel like I'm still firing on all cylinders.'

Daphne smirked. 'And two steak dinners.'

'Yes, well, I don't like to waste good food. You ate most of yours.'

Jefersen waved to them from the hotel entrance.

Daphne smoothed down her dress. 'He's waiting for us.'

He smiled as they approached.

'You both look lovely. I'm sure it's been a long day for you, so thanks for joining us tonight. Travis is in the lounge.'

Jefersen led the way and they were seated at a table by the window.

'What would you like to drink? Champagne?' Jefersen offered.

'Eh, that would be perfect,' said Daphne.

A bar waiter served their champagne and Jefersen proposed a toast.

'To friendship and love far from home.'

They tipped their glasses together and sipped their drinks.

'Where's John?' Ibbie asked.

'He's in Tiara's room,' said Jefersen. 'I told her we'd pick him up later and give him back to you. He's been amazing, getting into the fights and the action.'

'John's always been a scrapper,' Ibbie explained. 'That's why his fur is a bit uneven.'

'He must've been a cute kitten,' said Travis.

'I've only had him for three years. He walked into my shop not long after I opened it, made himself at home and he's stayed with me ever since.'

Travis tilted his head at her. 'So he just walked into your life and that was that?'

'Yes. I tried to find out about his original owner. I even put a postcard in the local newsagent shop asking if someone had lost him, but no one ever came looking for him. I'm glad because I think of him as mine, and he is now. The only thing I know for sure is that his name is John. He had a name tag on his collar. That's all it said. He answered to it right away.'

Jefersen had their glasses topped up with more champagne.

Daphne pretended to scold him. 'You're trying to get us tipsy.'

'We promise to be on our best behaviour,' said Jefersen.

Ibbie giggled. 'Daphne and I are making no such promise.'

Daphne glared at her.

'I'm just joking,' said Ibbie.

The four sat for a while trading light–hearted stories.

A few couples were up slow dancing to relaxing music.

Jefersen stood up and said to Daphne, 'Would you like to dance?'

She took his hand and let him lead her on to the dance floor.

Ibbie and Travis joined them.

Daphne's nervousness increased when she started to slow dance with Jefersen. He'd changed his dark shirt and now wore a white shirt, open at the neck. She felt the muscles in his shoulders beneath the fabric and had the overwhelming urge to wrap her arms around his neck and dance even closer to him.

She gazed up at him. Jeez he was stunning. As they danced, she wondered if Ibbie's theory was correct — was she better off taking a chance on love with someone she hadn't known for long? It certainly hadn't worked out being sensible. She'd tried and failed at that more times than she cared to remember.

'Having doubts?' Jefersen asked her, reading her expression.

'Just thinking about something Ibbie said.' She explained the theory.

'I like that theory. Anything that works in my favour of winning you over gets my vote.'

Travis and Ibbie danced by. 'What are we voting for?' said Travis.

'Ask Ibbie to explain about her romance theory,' suggested Jefersen.

Ibbie knew exactly what he meant, and proceeded to tell Travis as they waltzed on by.

'I hear you may be training with the stunt guys tomorrow morning,' Jefersen said with a grin.

'No, I'm going to be busy with the orders for the shop. I'm due a delivery of goldwork embroidery thread and wire and I've already got a backlog of orders for the items.'

'Goldwork? Sounds wonderful. What is it?'

'It's embroidery using metal thread.'

'I need to learn more about your work, Daphne.'

'Why? You're a film director not a dressmaker.'

'To learn more about you.'

Her heart squeezed at the thought that he cared to get to know her. Then just as she thought he was going to kiss her, a flash of lightning shone through the lounge windows, startling everyone.

'A summer rainstorm,' said Daphne. 'Ibbie and I better get back before it batters down.'

Jefersen nodded. 'You should get some sleep too, especially as it's an early start for you tomorrow.'

The evening in the lounge had been drawing to a close anyway, and although Daphne would've been happy to spend more time with Jefersen, she welcomed going home to gather her thoughts and to get some sleep.

Barra hurried over to them. 'The cat is asleep in Tiara's room and she doesn't want to disturb him, so is it okay for the kitty to stay here overnight?'

'Yes,' said Ibbie. 'I'll come and get him in the morning.'

Barra gave them the thumbs up and hurried away.

Ibbie followed Daphne out of the lounge.

'We'll walk you home,' said Jefersen.

Thunder roared in the distance and the scent of an impending storm filled the night air.

Daphne stood at the entrance and gazed out. Not a drop of rain yet, but they'd need to hurry before it poured down.

'No, it's fine,' Daphne assured them. 'We'll be okay.'

There was no point in rousing the crew to get one of them to drive them.

'I'll call a cab,' said Jefersen.

'We might have to wait ages,' said Daphne. 'If we hurry now we'll be there in a few minutes.'

Daphne and Ibbie hurried out into the night with the sound of thunder closer and louder this time.

Jefersen insisted on going with them, as did Travis.

The foursome walked briskly down the street heading to the dressmaking and knitting shops. Hardly anyone was about. The crowds who had taken part in the filming had gone home and anyone else had run for cover hearing the storm approach.

They'd almost reached the shops when the rain started.

Jefersen's white shirt was soaked as he shielded Daphne from the onslaught.

Shame on her, she thought to herself, for enjoying the feeling of his strong, lean torso, soaking wet, pressed hard against her, trying to protect her. The rain dripped off his hair and as she gazed up at him, the blond strands looked like liquid gold highlighted against the street lamps and lights from the shop windows. It felt as if time had slowed just for her as he leaned down and kissed her — a rain soaked kiss that she knew she'd remember forever.

His shirt was now completely soaked but he stood strong and didn't seem to care. He kept smiling at her, lovingly, sexily.

'I'll see you tomorrow, Daphne,' he promised, waiting until she was safely inside her shop, as he had done before.

Through the pouring rain she saw the blurred figures of Travis and Ibbie kissing goodnight too. The dark shirt Travis wore clung to his fit physique.

Daphne blinked away the rain and hurried inside her shop, hating having to shut Jefersen out, but he was smiling at her, giving her a reassuring wave that he was fine, and then he ran with Travis back up to the hotel.

Daphne went upstairs and peered out the window to get one last glance of Jefersen and Travis before they disappeared from view. She then stepped out of her wet dress, hung it up where it would dry, and got ready for bed.

A text popped up from Ibbie. *Great night, sleep tight, chat in the morning.*

Daphne reached over and knocked twice on the bedroom wall, signalling goodnight to Ibbie.

Lightning tore across the sky and Daphne kept the curtains open to watch it.

She tugged her patchwork quilt up, snuggled down to watch nature's spectacular summer rainstorm, and thought about kissing Jefersen.

CHAPTER TEN

Goldwork Embroidery

Daphne woke up at dawn the next morning and peered outside. Rain fell like mist casting everything in soft focus. She opened the window and breathed in the fresh air.

After breakfast she made an early start in the shop, wrapping orders that were picked up by courier, and unpacked a delivery of goldwork embroidery threads. In the haberdashery part of her shop she had a goldwork display selling everything from metallic threads and wires to beads and embroidery accessories.

Then she set about running up Tiara's dresses in the sewing machine. She'd already cut the pattern pieces and done some initial tacking so this allowed her to whiz along the seams and prepare the dresses for a fitting. Sewing two dresses was almost as easy as making one, especially as they were the same dress only in different colours. The fuchsia pink stitched up a treat and the black fabric created a chic little number. A bit of goldwork on the black dress would look wonderful. She thought she'd ask Tiara if she wanted this during the fitting.

She hung Tiara's dresses on a rail, and cut more fat quarters of the floral colouring book fabrics ready for sale. Then she added embroidery samples to her window display.

And all the while she thought about Jefersen. She couldn't get him out of her thoughts. Not that she wanted to.

As she was embroidering sweet pea flowers and lily of the valley as part of her display, she saw Barra going past the front window carrying John. He'd tucked the cat inside his jacket to keep him dry. Both of them glanced in at her. Barra waved and chapped on Ibbie's door.

Daphne stepped outside, sheltering under the flowery umbrella she kept near the entrance.

'Could you pass a message on to Tiara Timberlane for me?' she asked Barra.

'Yes, what do you want me to tell her?'

'Her dresses are ready for a fitting.'

'I'll let her know and ask her to give you a call.'

'Thank you. And did everything go okay with John's sleepover with her?'

'It did. Both of them slept sound and have been pampered rotten,' he said jokingly.

Ibbie opened up her shop and welcomed John in.

Barra waved and headed back to the hotel.

Daphne popped into the knitting shop and made tea while Ibbie fed John.

'I woke up early and couldn't stop thinking about last night — and Travis,' Ibbie confessed. 'So I came down and worked on knitting your cardigan. I feel edgy, needing to be busy.'

'I'm the same. Slightly calmer, but I've sewn Tiara's dresses and organised my goldwork embroidery display.'

'We should date men like Travis and Jefersen more often. We'd get a ton of work done and keep fit. I'm burning up everything I munch like a thoroughbred. And I feel bouncy, like I could take on the world, and I probably am. I glanced at my emails this morning. Other newspapers want to interview me, and you, and of course talk about John. Then there are loads of other folk wanting my attention, not customers, others interested in the film work, and I don't know who most of them are. I closed the laptop again and got on with knitting your cardigan. Talk about sticking your head in the sand, I'm sticking mine in a knitting pattern.'

Daphne laughed.

'You can laugh, but it's true.'

'I didn't feel like laughing when I walked downstairs to my shop early this morning,' said Daphne. 'The smirry rain muffled everything, it was so quiet, like the shop was wrapped up against the outside world, and I wasn't sure if I wanted to let it in. There's a safe feeling in familiarity. Sometimes the humdrum is comforting.'

'I know what you mean. When I went down to my shop I stood for a moment looking around. I thought, if I take things to the next level with Travis, everything in my wee shop will be gone. I felt so sad I almost wept, and yet. . .I think I'm going to have to let go of it. I'll regret it if I don't.'

Daphne sniffed. 'It is sad, isn't it?'

'Happy and sad. It's a double–edged sword we've cut for ourselves.'

'We'll stick together though, eh?'

'We always do, Daph, we always do.'

The kettle boiled and Daphne made the tea while Ibbie ran to Nairna's shop for the fresh baked morning rolls. The rain had stopped and the sun was starting to shine through the clouds. Steam rose from the pavements as the heat began to dry the wet street. Another warm day was assured.

Daphne set the tea tray up on the shop counter. She glanced at John, his tail up, enjoying his breakfast, content to be home. What would happen to John she wondered? Would Ibbie take him with her to Los Angeles? She didn't want to bring this up with Ibbie, not at the moment.

Ibbie came running back with a bag of four rolls. She held up another bag. 'I bought us two iced cream buns for our morning tea break.'

They sat together eating their buttered rolls, drinking tea and talking about Jefersen and Travis.

A short time later, Tiara arrived. She stepped inside the knitting shop wearing expensive cream trousers and a top and jacket two shades darker. Her hair was swept up in a chignon and her makeup was again perfection. A designer handbag dangled casually from her shoulder.

'Barra said the dresses are ready for a fitting. I'm busy later rehearsing scenes with Shaw, so could we do the fitting now?'

'Yes.'

Tiara followed Daphne next door after giving John a wave.

The dresses hung on a rail near the counter.

'They look lovely.' Tiara lifted the pink one off the rail.

'I don't have a proper changing room, but you can try it on in the sewing room. It's private and there's a mirror to see if you like it.'

Tiara smiled and went through to try it on.

Daphne locked the shop door to ensure they weren't interrupted.

'I love it,' Tiara called through to her.

Daphne peeked in.

Tiara smoothed her hands down the dress, happy with the feel of the fabric and the fit.

Daphne checked the shoulder fit and the seams. 'All it needs is the hem sewn up.'

They agreed on what length was suitable and Daphne pinned it up, measuring it exactly.

'Slip out of that one. Careful of the pins. I'll bring the black one through.'

Tiara tried the black dress on and was even more delighted. 'This is gorgeous. Such a great fit. Thank you, Daphne, for your quick work.'

'You're welcome.'

The hem was pinned up and Tiara changed into her original clothes.

'I wondered if you'd like any goldwork embroidery on the black dress?' Daphne showed her samples of what could be stitched on.

'The bee is gorgeous. I love bees.'

'How about a bumblebee, embroidered on like a brooch? I'll use gold and black threads and a bit of beading.'

'Yeah, do that. These motifs are so cool,' Tiara said, admiring the display. 'Could I have something on the pink dress?'

'Yes. Something shimmery but colourful would work well on the pink.'

'What do you suggest?'

'A sparkling butterfly or dragonfly.'

Daphne held up two embroidery patterns — outlines of the designs.

'I like the dragonfly, and I love butterflies.' She bit her lip. 'Can I have both? Would that work?'

'Yes, I could embroider one like a brooch and sew the other near the hem.'

'Great, I'll leave you to get on. Add whatever the cost is to the original payment for the extra work.'

'No, it's fine. I often add embellishments to the dresses I sell. It's part of my design work.'

'Yes, but—'

'Really. The cost is the same as it was.' Daphne smiled firmly.

Tiara seemed taken aback. 'Okay, Daphne. Thanks again.'

Tiara left the shop. Some of the film crew were setting up nearby and she headed over to them.

Daphne stitched the hems up so that all she had to do was embroider the motifs on.

Ibbie popped in and Daphne told her about Tiara's dresses.

Ibbie's green eyes lit up with interest. 'Embroidery? I never thought about that for my dress. I don't suppose. . .'

Daphne promised to embroider a little seahorse on Ibbie's pink dress. A seahorse in turquoise, pink, gold and lilac silk threads.

Daphne continued sewing throughout the morning. Local trade was slow because everyone was so involved in the filming, but her online sales had increased. This kept her busy but gave her more quiet time in her shop to embroider the dresses. She'd always enjoyed hand embroidery work and used a selection of stitches to create the designs.

Tiara phoned her at lunchtime. 'I told wardrobe about the dresses you've made, and as we're filming a scene down the beach this evening, would either of the dresses be finished in time for me to wear?'

'To wear in the film?' asked Daphne.

'Yes, they're preferable to the dresses I was scheduled to wear, and if you could do this I'd appreciate it.'

'I've been working on them and they'll definitely be ready for this evening.'

'Wonderful. I'll have someone from wardrobe pick them up. You'll be credited in the movie as my dressmaker.'

Daphne clicked the phone off and fought the urge to jump up and down. She ran to tell Ibbie.

'That's brilliant,' said Ibbie. 'We'll go down the shore and watch them filming tonight.'

Jefersen stopped by Daphne's shop in the late afternoon. They were alone in the shop and there was an intimacy between them that set her senses wild. He'd heard about Tiara's dresses, and Daphne showed him her handiwork.

'This is the bumblebee.' She held up the black dress.

'Very nice. I like it. So that's goldwork?'

'It is.'

He grinned. 'I'm learning.'

He had such a sexy smile she thought, feeling the colour rise in her cheeks. She then showed him the pink dress with the butterfly and dragonfly.

'Great work. I don't know if the filming will emphasise the embroidery details, but Tiara is pleased with the dresses and it's important that she feels fantastic in them. We're shooting a couple of romance scenes with Tiara and Shaw.' He stepped closer and gazed down at her. 'He's going to have to kiss her like he really cares.'

'I'm sure Shaw can manage that. He's a good actor and he seems to get along with Tiara.'

'There was a rumour they used to date, but it was just a rumour. But you're right, Shaw can act and he does get along with her. Their on–screen chemistry sizzles.'

He stepped closer again.

'Sizzles, huh?' she teased him.

He clasped his arms around her and pulled her close. 'Luckily, I don't need to act.'

Daphne gazed up at him. 'No?'

Jefersen shook his head and gave her a sexy grin that made her melt.

And then he leaned down and kissed her, gently at first and then with a passion that made her heart ache to be closer to him.

He finally stepped back. 'I better be going. Will you be at the shoot tonight?'

'Yes, I'll be there and so will Ibbie. John's not in the seashore scene so he'll be tucked up in his basket.'

'Afterwards, maybe we can have supper or a drink at the hotel. I feel we didn't get much chance last night to be together because of the rainstorm.'

'The forecast is threatening more rain late in the evening.'

He smiled at her, and his eyes shone with sincere affection. 'We can work around the rain. We can make things work if we want them to.'

'Are you always so optimistic?'

'I am when I'm around you.' He smiled again and then left.

She waved to him and he waved back.

She stood alone in the shop, watching him walk away, and then he disappeared into the crowd of film crew and others working on a scene further along the road.

She glanced around her shop. What did she want? The security of her little dressmaking shop in Scotland? Or the chance of a happy life in Hollywood with Jefersen?

She had less than two weeks to make up her mind.

The sweeping bay with its sparkling silvery sea looked beautiful in the evening light. Jefersen and Travis were busy organising the shoot. The film crew had set up their cameras and lighting along parts of the shore with the sea in the background. The tide was out, allowing them access to the long stretch of golden sand. The air was calm and warm, and the shore had retained the heat from the hot summer day.

Daphne and Ibbie watched the activity from the esplanade, as did numerous others from the town. The twilight sky glowed deep turquoise, pink and lilac, merging with the fading amber light along the horizon. The low outline of the islands far in the distance added to the beauty of the scenery. There was nothing rugged about this area of the coast.

'The shore looks gorgeous,' said Ibbie. 'Jefersen will make this look spectacular.'

Daphne agreed. 'We don't come down here often enough. It really is quite beautiful.'

'We're always too busy working or knackered in the evenings.' Ibbie paused and then pointed. 'Oh look, there's Tiara wearing one of your dresses. She suits it. It shows off her figure.'

Tiara wore the pink dress looking like they'd deliberately matched it to the sky. Shaw wore dark colours, a handsome silhouette, but his blond hair stood out against the backdrop. He was talking to Travis and holding a script. They appeared to be going over part of it.

Jefersen peered through one of the cameras and panned along the shoreline. As he gave the thumbs up to the crew, they got ready to film part of the romance scene.

Just before the cameras rolled, Jefersen looked up to the esplanade, searching the faces in the crowd, and waved when he saw Daphne and Ibbie. Daphne wore a vintage print dress with sandals, and Ibbie had opted for a similar look with a multicoloured print. They waved back to him.

The filming began with Shaw and Tiara strolling along the beach chatting. Shaw paused and clasped hold of Tiara, pulling her towards him for a passionate kiss. They kissed for a few moments and then Jefersen shouted, 'Cut.'

Jefersen went over to the actors and discussed aspects of the story with them while the cameras were set to reshoot the scene.

'They acted that scene well,' Ibbie commented. 'But it must be weird having to kiss someone you don't fancy.'

'Yes, it must be hard kissing Shaw Starlight.' Daphne smirked at Ibbie.

'Very funny. Okay, so I used to fancy the pants off him, and there are worse jobs than smooching Shaw, but you know fine what I mean.'

'You'd rather smooch Travis.'

'Just as you'd prefer to snog Jefersen, and have done, very recently if Ivy's gossip is correct.'

'What gossip?'

'Ivy walked past your shop this afternoon. She was going to pop in for embroidery thread, but you were locking lips solid with Jefersen. Lost to the world. She watched for a few moments, thinking you'd surely let him go, but oh no, you were too busy smooching.'

'I suppose she's told all the sewing bee ladies.'

'There's no suppose about it. That's how I heard. Ivy told Florie who told June, then it looped to Effie and she phoned me.'

'No secrets in this town.'

'Never has been, Daphne. That's what makes it fun.'

'Speaking of fun. . . the stuntmen are rollicking along the sand.'

Ibbie looked at them. 'Effie said they were practising lots of energetic moves down the shore today. This must've been what it was for.'

Daphne glanced over at Effie and Ivy's cottages and saw them watching everything from their windows. She waved to them and they signalled back.

Moments later, Ivy's cottage door opened and Florie came running across to Daphne and Ibbie.

'We've just made tea. Come up for a cuppa. There's a great view of the filming from our windows.'

They followed Florie back to the cottage in time to help Effie carry in two trays of cupcakes she'd hurriedly swirled with buttercream.

'Thanks, girls. I baked these up quick so we could have them while watching the romance scene.' Effie winked at Daphne. 'Though I heard you were helping Jefersen rehearse some kissing in your shop. Giving him ideas for the film were you?' She giggled.

Daphne grabbed a tray of cupcakes. 'I bet I could be upstairs in my kitchen doing a can–can dance and someone would gossip about it.'

Effie shrugged. 'Your kitchen window looks on to the street. Someone would see your high–kicking and tell the town.'

Giggling and joking, they headed into Ivy's cottage where the table was set for tea beside the window.

'Tiara looks like a model in that dress, Daphne,' said Ivy.

'Have you seen her designer handbags?' Florie sighed. 'They're fabulous. She's got two tonight hanging on the back of her chair.'

They all peered out the window.

Chairs for the film crew were set on the sand. Tiara's canvas chair with her name across the back had two voluminous handbags slung on it. It was too far to view the details, but according to Florie who had seen Tiara walk past earlier with them, they were worth a mint.

'Tiara is one of the top stars in Hollywood so she can afford to be lavish,' said Effie.

The ladies agreed, and watched the action being filmed while enjoying their tea and cakes.

Ivy then exchanged a nod with Florie, before speaking up.

'There's never going to be an appropriate time to bring this subject up,' Ivy said to Daphne and Ibbie.

Everyone stopped drinking their tea as Ivy continued. 'We've always been straightforward with each other, so. . . if you two decide to go to Los Angeles with Jefersen and Travis, Florie and I are interested in taking on the lease of your dressmaking shop. And Effie and several of the sewing bee members want to take on Ibbie's knitting shop. We'll all combine our resources, financial and sewing expertise, to turn the two shops into sewing bee shops selling fabric, dresses, expand the haberdashery part and include knitting yarn, but focus more on sewing, including quilting and embroidery. A real sewing bee venture.'

Daphne and Ibbie were completely taken aback. Ivy had worded it well, but they were momentarily caught unawares.

'And if you can't take John with you to Hollywood, Ibbie, we'll look after him and love him on your behalf,' Ivy added. 'He'll be safe and happy with us.'

At the thought of having to leave John behind, Ibbie burst into tears.

The women comforted her.

'I'm sorry,' Ivy apologised, 'I shouldn't have brought it up.'

Ibbie sniffled into a hankie. 'No, Ivy, you're right. I'm just feeling overly emotional.'

Daphne's eyes welled up, but she managed to keep a grip on her emotions. 'Ibbie and I have spoken about leaving our shops, and how upsetting it would be. But we also realise that if there's a chance of happiness for us in Hollywood, we should take it.'

'I know you've only started to get involved with Jefersen and Travis,' said Effie, 'but we can all see how well you get on. We've seen various engagements and marriages in this town to know when a couple suit each other.'

Florie spoke up. 'I love my quilt shop so I can understand how difficult it would be to let it go. I'm a homebody at heart and could never leave here. Scotland is where I belong. But the two of you, even if we've never told you, have always aimed for the stars. You're the type who could make a new life for yourselves in Hollywood.'

'At least our shops wouldn't be closed or turned into something else,' said Daphne. 'It's heartening knowing the sewing bee would take them over.'

'And think of the holidays we could all have with you,' said Effie. 'I've never been to America. I've always fancied going but never have.'

'I'm the same,' said Ivy. 'It would be another adventure for all of us.'

'I've been to New York,' June told them. 'I enjoyed it, but I've never visited the west coast. The sunshine in California would be lovely.' Then she added, 'I work at the bakery, but I'd jump at the chance to work in the sewing bee shops. Being surrounded with lots of fabric, patterns, threads and craft stuff would be my idea of job perfection.'

'With all of us working in the shops, we'd be able to pop over for a visit while the others looked after the business,' said Florie.

Ivy made another round of tea and they continued to chat about their plans while watching the filming out the window.

A text message came through for Daphne from Jefersen. *We're finishing the filming for tonight. Got some great shots. The shore is perfect. Want to come down? Tiara wants to talk to you.*

Daphne replied. *We're on our way.*

Ibbie and Daphne headed down on to the sand where the film crew were packing up.

Tiara sat on her chair, and got up when she saw Daphne and waved her over.

As Daphne and Ibbie approached, Tiara lifted one of the handbags from her chair and thrust it at Daphne.

'I've only used this bag for like five minutes ever,' said Tiara. 'I want you to have it.'

Daphne blinked. 'But I—'

'Take it. I insist. You won't accept money for the embroidery work on the dresses. Most people would've taken advantage, but you didn't, so I thought you may like this.'

Daphne accepted the designer handbag, feeling the quality of it, loving it instantly. 'Thank you. That's very kind.'

'Kindness deserves kindness.' Tiara smiled and then let herself be swept away by the wardrobe assistants up to the esplanade where transport was waiting to whisk her to the hotel.

Daphne looked at the bag and then at Ibbie.

'Wowsa!' Ibbie gasped. 'What a pressie. But you deserve it for all the work you put into her dresses. And you did bother to make them special and didn't rip her off financially even though she's wealthy.'

Daphne slung the strap of the bag up on her shoulder. 'Oh yes, this is a beaut.'

'Hey! I've been looking for you,' Travis called to Ibbie, bounding over to welcome her. 'It's such a nice evening. Would you care to go for a walk along the beach?'

Ibbie linked her arm through his, and cast a mischievous smile over her shoulder at Daphne.

Daphne gave her a little wave.

'Jefersen and I were wondering where you were,' said Travis, gazing down at her as they walked along. Then he peered closely. 'Have you been crying? Did someone upset you?'

Ibbie let it all spill out, her concerns about leaving, especially John.

Travis stopped and clasped her firmly by the shoulders. 'John's coming with us,' he said as if the alternative had never crossed his mind. 'We're not leaving that little guy behind.'

Ibbie jumped up and threw her arms around Travis' neck and hugged the breath out of him. And then they walked on along the shore, arms wrapped around each other.

'They look happy,' Jefersen said over Daphne's shoulder.

She spun around. 'Oh, you startled me.'

'Sorry.'

'No, it's fine, I was just lost in thought and watching Ibbie with Travis.' She explained about John, guessing that's what her friend had been so happy about.

'John's adaptable, and he loves the sunshine, so he'll have plenty of that in L.A. Travis has a real nice house with a garden.' He grinned at her. 'And a pool, just in case you were wondering.'

'For as long as I've known Ibbie she's loved reading about all the Hollywood celebrity gossip and keeps up with the latest films. She belongs in the world she's always dreamed about rather than here.'

'Hopefully, she's not the only one.' His eyes twinkled in the twilight's glow and he was the most handsome she'd ever seen him. Standing there with him on the sand with everyone having drifted off home or to the hotel felt magical. The sea sparkled behind him and the air was so calm she could hear her own breathing increase with the excitement she felt building inside her.

Jefersen kissed her, put his arm around her shoulders, and they walked along the shore in the opposite direction, giving Ibbie and Travis privacy and time to be alone.

Daphne was alone now too with Jefersen.

'Can I carry your bag for you?' he offered.

'I'll hold on to it,' she said, clutching the bag close to her.

He laughed at this, joking with her, kissing her again and then walking along the shore.

During the next two weeks, Daphne and Ibbie spent more and more time with Jefersen and Travis, taking their relationships to the next level and the next, until the thought of being apart when it came time for them and the film crew to leave the town was unbearable.

Jefersen spoke about Daphne's dressmaking skills, encouraging her to continue with her career in Los Angeles along with Ibbie.

'Though I don't know if Hollywood is ready for you two,' Jefersen said with a smile.

The filming in Scotland had received excellent publicity and from the way the footage was coming together, the crew knew it was going to be a success. Jefersen planned to cut an early trailer of the movie and include John's action scenes in it. More publicity was assured. Everyone was happy with the outcome, including Shaw and Tiara.

Plans were made to hand over the shop leases to the sewing bee ladies. Unknown to them, Jefersen prepaid six months rent for them as a parting gift for all they'd done. The paperwork for the shops, passports and every aspect including taking John with them were dealt with.

On the morning Daphne and Ibbie were due to leave their old lives behind and fly off to Los Angeles with Jefersen and Travis, they took a final look around each other's shops. A few tears of regret and happiness were shed, lots of reassuring hugs, a couple of mementos of their time in the shops slipped into their handbags, and the keys left on the counters.

They'd already said their goodbyes to the sewing bee ladies. Hew had waved across at Daphne early that morning. He didn't come over or say farewell. He didn't need to. The look that passed between them said it all. Hew deserved someone who loved him dearly, and she wished him well.

Daphne and Ibbie stood one last time in the dress shop.

'I can't believe we're really going to do this,' said Daphne. Chills of excitement ran through her, causing her to shiver with a mix of trepidation and then blush bright pink with anticipation of the new life awaiting her with Jefersen in his gorgeous houses in Los Angeles. He'd made several promises to her and she believed he'd keep them all. One included taking their relationship to the highest level and choosing a diamond ring when she felt ready. Promises he made. And kept.

Ibbie squeezed hold of Daphne's arm. 'We are, we're going to Hollywood. It's all waiting for us there.' Travis had made similar promises to Ibbie. In her dreams she pictured a pretty diamond ring, representing their future together. She'd never been more sure of anything. And Travis kept those promises too.

With a final glance around the dress shop, Daphne and Ibbie clasped hands for strength and hope, and stepped away from their past and forward to a whole new happy future in Hollywood.

End

Now that you've read the story, you can try your hand at colouring in the illustrations.

De-ann has been writing, sewing, knitting, quilting, gardening and creating art and designs since she was a little girl. Writing, dressmaking, knitting, quilting, embroidery, gardening, baking cakes and art and design have always been part of her world.

About the Author:

De-ann Black is a bestselling author, scriptwriter and former newspaper journalist. She has over 50 books published. Romance, crime thrillers, espionage novels, action adventure. And children's books (non-fiction rocket science books and children's fiction).

She previously worked as a full-time newspaper journalist for several years. She had her own weekly columns in the press. This included being a motoring correspondent where she got to test drive cars every week for the press for three years.

Before being asked to work for the press, De-ann worked in magazine editorial writing everything from fashion features to social news. She was the marketing editor of a glossy magazine. She is also a professional artist and illustrator. Fabric design, dressmaking, sewing, knitting and fashion are part of her work.

Additionally, De-ann has always been interested in fitness, and was a fitness and bodybuilding champion, 100 metre runner and mountaineer. As a former N.A.B.B.A. Miss Scotland, she had a weekly fitness show on the radio that ran for over three years.

De-ann trained in Shukokai karate, boxing, kickboxing, Dayan Qigong and Jiu Jitsu. She is currently based in Scotland.

Her colouring books are available in paperback. Find out more at: www.de-annblack.com